*Inspiration*

---

*Inspiration*

---

Stephanie Ash

**X**
LIBRIS

An *X Libris* Book

First published by X Libris in 1995

A CIP catalogue record for this book
is available from the British Library.

ISBN 0 7515 1489 6

Photoset in North Wales by
Derek Doyle & Associates, Mold, Clwyd
Printed and bound in Great Britain by
Clays Ltd, St Ives plc

X Libris
A Division of
Little, Brown and Company (UK)
Brettenham House
Lancaster Place
London WC2E 7EN

*To Angélique,*
*who taught me*
*all I know.*

1

# Inspiration

# Chapter One

BEAUTY ARTICLES IN glossy magazines always say that the best way to match a foundation to your skin is to try it out directly on your face, rather than on your wrist where the skin is, quite simply, a totally different colour. It's a great theory, Clare thought, applying the rules of Max Factor to the medium of Monet, as she daubed a little more paint on to her model's cheeks. He twitched nervously – and excitedly, she hoped, since it wasn't the cheeks of his face that she was trying to match.

'That's cold,' he complained.

'Perfect,' Clare exclaimed, ignoring her model's little moans. She dashed back to her canvas with palette in hand and added another sweeping stroke to her latest nude. They were selling like hot cakes. Flying out of the studio to be hung on the walls of the rich, famous and voyeuristic.

'Stunningly realistic,' said the reviews. 'Remarkable use of colour.' And quite right too. She wouldn't have imagined that there were many

1

artists who would go to such great lengths to perfectly match a skin tone.

'Just one more session and then I think we'll be finished, Michael,' Clare told the model as she neared him and his beautifully tanned buttocks quivered expectantly. 'It's OK. I think I've mixed enough paint now.' Was that a sigh of disappointment she heard? 'Well, I suppose I could always . . .'

Clare traced a line down her model's back, from the nape of his neck, right down his left leg, with a soft clean brush. When she reached his strong, brown calves, he slowly rolled over so that he was lying on his back, ready for her to continue her journey. As she drew the brush along his instep his toes scrunched in delight.

'That tickles,' he moaned.

'I'll show you what tickles,' Clare told him, a devilish glint in her eyes.

She threw the brush down on to the floor and clambered on to the couch so that she was balancing precariously at its end. Where the brush had left off, she picked up with her tongue, circling the bone of his ankle before attempting to find the least hairy path up his shin to his thigh.

Softly, softly. Clare held her long dark hair out of the way so that the only part of her that touched him was the tip of her tongue. Every slow inch or so she took a break and looked up to see his reaction. His eyes were shut. Eyebrows raised in a gesture of pleasure. But when he felt she had been looking and not licking for too long, he opened his eyes to implore her to continue. And what incredible eyes they were. Green flecked with ginger, like the eyes of some kind of mythical creature that had just come in from the woods.

Clare's eyes met his. Then his gaze dropped to something which was starting to come between them.

'Do, please, carry on,' he murmured with a smile.

She didn't need asking twice.

Clare lowered herself back on to her path and it wasn't long before she found that it was going vertical. She rested a while. The tip of her tongue hovering at that spot where the balls join the dick. His hips skewed slightly to one side, then he dropped one leg off the couch so that she was able to settle herself into a more comfortable position to finish what she had started.

The model ran a hand through his thick tawny hair, then wiped away the sweat that had begun to gather on his brow. Clare liked to have her studio hot. A single dewy bead glistened at the eye of his penis. She longed to know if he tasted as good as he looked. Like a chameleon, she flicked out her tongue and hit the spot. An involuntary groan of delight escaped his lips.

Having reached her destination, Clare decided that it was about time she backed up the work of her tongue with her hands and wrapped her paint-smeared fingers around his now impressively large shaft. But her model was tired of this one-sided teasing. Suddenly, he had risen from his prone position and it was Clare who was on her back, her head dangling over the end of the chaise longue, throwing her throat open to his

3

expertly light kisses. Deftly he unfastened the silk kimono which she always wore to paint since it gave her such freedom of movement. For a moment, he merely appreciated the view.

'You are so gorgeous,' he breathed, running a soft hand along the pale pink contours before him.

On the wooden floor beside the couch was a bottle of olive oil that Clare used to add to her oil paints from time to time to give them a slightly smoother texture. As her arm dropped from the side of the chaise longue, her hand brushed against it. Involuntarily she looked towards it. But it was too late, her model had spotted the bottle too and Clare rolled her eyes as he picked it up and began to pour a little of the viscous golden liquid into the palm of his hand.

'Warm that up!' she demanded. Too late. His hand came face down on her belly and she breathed in sharply at the shock of the cold virgin oil against her skin. But it was quickly abated as he slid his hand around in a circle three or four times to spread the oil out. He looked deep in thought for a moment and she shivered as he drew a finger across the shiny surface he had made of her skin. He drew a line from her breastbone to her navel, which ended in a quick exploratory dip into that oil-filled orifice.

Then, ever so slowly, he began to slide both palms up the centre of her body, spreading them out when he reached her breasts, smearing the oil all over them so that they shone like burnished bronze. An involuntary moan escaped her lips as his palms brushed lightly over her fast firming nipples. And then he was moving down, down. Drawing his hands back over her belly and down to her thighs, one hand on each, wrapping his fingers around their curving muscles. Long, fast, hard strokes from her hips to her ankles made the blood begin to zing around her lower body.

Clare was covered now from neck to toe, shining with oil, and the beginnings of a sweat as the feel of his hands and the sight of his concentrated expression aroused her circulation in all the right areas. He, too, was glowing.

'Feeling good?' he asked.

She nodded.

His hands were steadily creeping up the insides of her satiny, glistening thighs, which tensed with anticipation. He stopped, the tips of his thumbs just an inch or so away from her lips. Their eyes locked again, his narrowing with mischief. As her thighs tensed, when he moved his hands ever closer to her vagina, she felt her own wetness, oozing out on to her skin.

'Aaaah.'

He slipped a single finger into her vagina. The delicious sensation of penetration. The walls of her vagina rippled in pleasurable reply to his gentle thrustings. As he thrust, he stretched up to kiss her, first on one nipple and then the other. Sucking each hard, pink bud into his mouth until she felt the pressure of his teeth and it almost hurt. Between his kissing lips and thrusting finger, her body was alive with sensation.

Then he moved up Clare's body, taking his hand from her pussy and instead cupping it beneath her head, to stop her from falling off the

5

couch. His body was now full length on top of hers. As he shifted position, she could hear little slurping, sticking sounds, of the oil between them. His neglected penis now lay impatiently between her closed thighs. She opened them awkwardly beneath his weight and his dick sprang into the gap like a missile dropping from the hatch of a bomber. He was still kissing her mouth, licking it, biting it gently, as he rocked and ground his slim hips against hers and his still stiffening dick nudged at her other lips.

'Can I?' he asked, gazing into her eyes. His pupils were so dilated with desire that his green eyes looked almost all black. Clare nodded slowly, and slid her hands around to his buttocks. Even as she was nodding, she could feel him suddenly increase the pressure of his rocking against her body. She opened her legs wider still and pressed his body towards hers.

'Aaaah.' The first thrust. The magical feeling of yielding to pleasure. Clare held him tight to her for a moment, to stop him from moving again while she savoured the sensation of the first thrust of their first fuck.


The ringing of the telephone broke Clare's concentration – and burst the bubble of her daydream. The luscious nude she had been painting in her mind once again became a washed out sea-scape. Her buttock palette, an old plastic egg box. She quickly wiped her paint smeared hands on the seat of her jeans and dashed from the studio into the lounge to take the call.

6

'Hello,' she trilled, full of expectation.

'Well, hellooo darling,' replied the caller. 'It's Graham from the Dragon Gallery.' That much Clare had already guessed. The sigh that she now exhaled as she shifted the phone to her other ear was definitely one of disappointment.

'What's up with you?' Graham asked.

'Just tired.'

'Up all night, eh?' His laugh made Clare feel as though someone was tying her insides in a knot.

'I wish.'

The dirty laugh again.

'What do you want, Graham?' She tried not to sound irritated.

'I've sold six of your paintings this week . . . To an American woman who wanted to take a little piece of England back to all her friends. She wants some more, as well. She's got a gallery in Houston. She reckons she can take at least twenty. They've got money to burn, those Yanks.'

'Cheers, Graham, I happen to think my work is worth buying.'

'Oh, I didn't mean it like that. You know I think you're priceless. You can come in and collect the money whenever you want. Or if you can't make it in during the day perhaps . . .'

The last thing Clare wanted was to see Graham from the Dragon Gallery during the hours of darkness, so she quickly said, 'I'll pop in just before lunch.'

'Lunch – that'd be great.'

'Lunch with Daniel,' she added, firmly.

'Haven't you got rid of him yet?'

'When I do, you'll be the first to know.'

'Oh well,' more sighs of disappointment. 'I'll see you in a bit, then.' Graham hung up. Clare felt like washing the ear that had been next to the receiver.

'Who was that?'

'Good afternoon, Daniel!'

Rip Van Winkle had finally awoken. Daniel, Clare's boyfriend, stood at the door of their bedroom, rubbing his eyes.

'Graham from The Dragon.'

Daniel made a face that echoed her feelings about the gallery owner who was definitely more interested in seeing her panties than her paintings. 'What did he want?' asked Daniel.

'He sold six paintings this week. Two of them big ones. That means we can get the car fixed.'

'That's great, really great . . . Did he sell any of mine?'

She shook her head.

'Oh.' A shadow of jealousy passed quickly across his face to be replaced by a slightly strained smile. 'Hey, well, I guess I'm just following in the footsteps of Van Gogh. I'll sell for millions when I'm dead.'

There was no laughter in Daniel's voice as he told his self-mocking joke.

'Come back to bed,' he said, curling his arms around Clare's waist and nestling his face in her shoulder. She squeezed him back momentarily. 'You look like you need a good fuck.'

Clare blushed. She was probably still flushed from her day-dream. 'I've got to get some paintings done,' she told Daniel as she unwrapped his arms from her body. They sprang back, in a tighter grip. Daniel nuzzled more ardently.

'Work later . . . later,' he whispered.

'No,' Clare protested. 'Work now.' Daniel was tousled and smelly from eleven hours sleep. 'I've got to do this now. The American woman who bought those paintings wants some more, for her own gallery back in the States. It could be the start of something big.'

'So could this,' Daniel pulled her hand down to the front of his shorts where the cotton was beginning to stretch and tighten over his hardening dick.

'I'll wake you up for lunch,' Clare said, wrestling her hand away. She popped herself out of his arms and fled towards the studio they had made of the spare room. Daniel didn't make it back to bed either. Grumbling, he slumped down on to the sofa and flicked on the TV.

Clare made her living as an artist. Her boyfriend Daniel was an artist as well – probably a better one than she, but about as commercial as an electric blanket in Death Valley. They had met at art school, getting together almost as soon as they started their course, and had been together ever since. Clare had been captivated by Daniel's brilliance, his originality, his imagination, which was as evident in him as it was in his pictures. And he also had a great body, well-muscled and lithe, usually clothed in black; he had dark, wildly curling hair and pale grey-blue eyes like those of a timber wolf . . . She sometimes thought that he had hypnotised her into bed with him.

After leaving college they moved to St Ives. For the light of course. The perfect light for painting which tempted so many people, who should have stuck to painting their dining room walls magnolia, to hang up the rat race for a stipple brush. Fresh out of college, they were used to being penniless and keen to continue being penniless in somewhere a little less polluted and materialistic than London.

Money doesn't matter to us, they would tell each other while they were still at college. We only need our artistic integrity . . . and each other. One or the other of them always seemed to add that as an afterthought. They were fiercely independent of each other, or at least it was fashionable to appear that way, but secretly Clare was overjoyed at the prospect of being in a strange town where she knew nobody but Daniel, the man of her dreams. Where they had only each other for company. And she thought that he was too. He needed her more than he could have admitted, she was sure.

The first few weeks, perhaps even the first two months, in Cornwall passed in a happy whirlwind of coastal walks and Cornish pasties. The sun shone. It was the hottest summer in four years. And both Clare and Daniel found part-time work very easily. Clare waited tables in one of the nicer guesthouses while Daniel pulled pints in the pub next door. By the time Clare had finished serving dinner and washing up, it would almost be time for Daniel to finish his shift too. She would wait for him in the corner of the lounge, sipping an orange juice, watching him work, listening to the happy chat of holiday makers and thanking her lucky stars that she had ended up in

Cornwall with him, rather than in London, slogging her guts out, designing silly patterns on cheap material to be turned into cheap dresses for a cheap chain store or painting fluffy animals on to cheesy birthday cards like so many of their art college friends.

But so much for artistic integrity. They certainly didn't paint much in those first two months. Just sleeping, serving in the restaurant . . . oh, and having sex. The novelty of their own flat, with a double bed! They had to make up for three years of sharing hot, restless nights in one of their single beds in the halls of residence. Hot and restless because the beds were too damn small and creaked too loudly, next to walls too paper thin to allow them to really let go when they were making love.

Oh, the joy of being able to moan in pleasure and know that you wouldn't have to face the textiles student in the room next door doing an impression of your passion over breakfast! One particular prat, called Darren, was always quoting clichés shouted at the height of passion. A girl on Clare's floor would always regret having screamed 'Oooh, baby, you're the pneumatic drill and I'm the pavement,' though Clare thought it was stranger that nobody asked Darren how he managed to glean all these gems of aural sex!

Anyway, the first two months in St Ives were great. But then the summer ended.

Daniel lost his job first. The landlord had warned him that it would only be for the summer, though Daniel had hoped that he might be kept

11

on when the tourists went home. But the recession had bitten badly. Unfortunately, it was a case of last in, first out. As for Clare, she lasted just a little longer at the hotel, but as soon as the 'Vacancies' sign went up in the window again, she was looking for a vacancy of a different sort.

Never mind, they consoled each other. They had saved a little money. Clare had done quite well for tips and had been carefully banking them at the end of every week. They'd sign on. They'd get by. After all – hadn't they come to St Ives to paint? To follow a vocation?

Daniel took up his brushes with a vengeance. The passion that they had recently shared in bed exploded on to his canvasses in bold swathes of blood red and roman candle explosions of orange and yellow.

But those pictures, the pictures that Daniel and Clare wanted to work on, canvasses that meant something to them, just weren't going to sell in this town. Joe Public would probably pronounce them a 'bit too modern for my tastes'. They wanted something to remind them of their holidays; a nice landscape, fishing boats by the sea. Something that would look 'very nice thank you' on their apple white walls and not grab them by the throat when they were walking around the house bleary-eyed in the morning.

So Clare painted some 'very nice thank you' stuff, while Daniel insisted on grabbing throats and Clare's fishing boats sailed out of the galleries, while his red, black and raucous canvasses stayed firmly put, week after week after week. Daniel accused Clare of having sold out . . . and she paid the rent.

Daniel was still lying on the sofa, snoring gently, when Clare emerged from their makeshift spare bedroom studio two hours after Graham's call. She flicked the TV off. If he awoke to the sound of the Neighbours theme tune he would watch that, and then Home and Away, then two or three quiz shows, and then the children's programmes, but if he woke up and the TV wasn't on, he might just be tempted to pick up a paintbrush instead.

Clare smoothed his fringe away from his sleeping eyes. He smiled in his dreams. He was still the most beautiful man she had ever seen.

# Chapter Two

THE DRAGON GALLERY was just about the best place to have your work displayed in town, next to the new Tate of course. It was near enough to that more famous gallery to ensure a steady flow of customers who were slightly more interested in art than average and therefore slightly more willing than average to pay for it.

Graham, the gallery owner, greeted Clare with that grin of his that always made her queasy. He held out the money from the sale of her paintings in a brown envelope and moved it backwards as she reached for it, forcing her to topple forwards so that her nose ended up buried in his sleeveless maroon jumper.

'Oops,' he exclaimed, helping Clare regain her balance by pushing her upright by the tits. Clare brushed herself off, snatched the money and tried to laugh light-heartedly. She couldn't afford to have him put up his commission for the sake of a little painful flirtation.

She counted out the money.

'Don't you trust me?' he asked, slipping an arm around her squirming waist.

'I don't trust myself when I'm near you, Graham,' Clare quipped. He seemed pleased. Money counted, she slipped it back into the envelope and then into her bag. She gave a 'see you when I see you' kind of wave and started to make for the door.

'Hang on,' he called, 'I need you to sign something to say that you've had the money and I've also got something rather special to give you, oo-er.'

Clare cringed and stopped, but waited right by the door, holding it slightly ajar, ready to make a quick getaway. Graham scribbled a makeshift receipt.

'So, how's your boyfriend?' he couldn't help asking as he wrote.

'Fine.'

'Where's he taking you for lunch?'

'Somewhere romantic.'

'So you're not planning to leave him and come and live with me yet?'

'No,' Clare said flatly, adding to keep him sweet, 'At least, not until you leave your wife.' She was studying Graham's thinning hair. He was mesmerisingly ugly. Everything in the wrong proportions. He looked like the FA Cup. In fact the only thing right about him was the number of eyes he had. As she focused on a lightly hairy mole on the side of his neck Clare remembered a girl at college who had read in a psychology book that if you look at anyone, and that is absolutely anyone, for long enough you will find yourself falling in love with them . . .

'Hey dreamer,' Graham purred. He had caught her looking at him, studying his neck. He probably thought she was sizing him up for a love bite. A little self-consciously he ran his fingers through what remained of his hair. He proffered the receipt and Clare signed it with the flourish that she would one day use to sign limited edition prints of the biceps and buttocks of the rich and famous. 'Well . . . don't spend it all at once!' Graham joked, 'unless you're stocking up on sexy undies for me.' Clare groaned. 'And I'd like a couple more of those water colour harbour pictures, if you have the time.'

'For you, Graham, I'll make the time.'

'Hey, don't forget this.' He handed her a small white envelope. She opened it and drew out a white card, with the dragon logo of the gallery embossed upon it in gold. 'The gallery's been open for ten years, so I'm having a party on Thursday to celebrate. You know, champagne and caviar! I'd like you to come . . . In fact, I'd love you to come.' He placed unnecessary emphasis on that last word.

'Mmm,' Clare thought, 'a party at the Dragon Gallery? Great venue. Champagne and caviar? Wonderful. But champagne and Graham? That could be a dangerous combination.' She'd probably have to have toothache on Thursday night instead.

'The wife is going to be at her mother's,' he added.

Did he think that was an incentive? Clare would definitely have toothache that evening now! But instead she told him, 'I'll try and be there . . . And I'll bring Daniel too, if that's OK?'

Graham sighed. 'I suppose so. Have a nice romantic lunch. Maybe one day I'll show you what romance is really about.'

Clare stepped out of the gallery laughing but her good mood didn't last long. Romance! What a joke. At best, her romantic lunch was going to be a couple of salad cream sandwiches at a paint-covered table, opposite a guy who, having given up on painting, was now determined to make sulking an art-form. She was nearing the flat, one hand on the front gate, the other in her pocket searching for her key, when she decided, 'Sod this!' Clare was going to treat herself. She glanced up at the window. She couldn't see Daniel so she figured that he hadn't seen her nearly arrive home. Clare would go to the vegetarian restaurant by the harbour that she had drooled over so many times, and then she would go and get her hair done, and a facial, and perhaps even a manicure. She had the cash in her pocket. If she went home now she would end up going to the pub with Daniel, to drown his sorrows with her money.

Clare closed the gate carefully and quietly with a bit of a sigh. It didn't seem that long ago that she wouldn't have dreamt of not wanting to spend lunch time, or any time, with Daniel. She remembered her birthday a year earlier, when he had surprised her with a champagne picnic lunch in Hyde Park. Even though it had begun to rain cats and dogs just seconds after they opened the first bottle, they hadn't minded. They had turned the picnic blanket into a rather ineffective tent and spent the afternoon beneath it, kissing, cuddling and catching colds.

It was hard to imagine that the Daniel she had left behind at the flat that morning was the same guy. Cornwall wasn't working out for him. Clare loved it. She was inspired. But she thought that perhaps Daniel felt dampened. Depressed by the lack of insight people here in Cornwall were showing into the way he painted. He needed to be in London. But she didn't need to have him taking out his frustrations on her.

Clare tried to put her worries about Daniel out of her mind.

On the way to the café she swung by the newsagents and picked up a glossy magazine so that she could pick a new hairstyle while she ate her lunch. She flicked through it as she walked along, reading the headlines.

'Every woman deserves a sexual adventure!' screamed the big pink letters on page five.

'My sentiments exactly,' she heard herself exclaim to the gulls wheeling in the grey sky.

In the tourist season Clare would have had to queue for about three days to get a seat in the haven of dried flowers and Viennese blinds that was Muffin's, but now, in October, it was almost empty. Two elderly ladies with hair dyed to match their pastel outfits sat at the best table in the window. There was just one other customer, towards the back of the shop. A guy, about thirty-five, reading a paper, looking incongruously sophisticated against the tea-shoppe kitsch.

The waitress placed a double espresso in front of him, smiling widely as she did so. He looked up briefly to thank her and Clare couldn't help straining over the refrigeration cabinet which blocked her view to see if his face lived up to the overall impression, which, for a man in St Ives outside the holiday season, was not bad at all.

'What do you want, love?' the woman behind the counter asked Clare as she was in mid gawp. Embarrassed, Clare looked back to the cabinet and picked out a pasta salad, which looked reasonably healthy, and a large piece of strawberry shortcake to reward herself for being so restrained in her first choice. And a cappuccino. As the woman behind the counter revved up the coffee machine and poured that out, Clare glanced around the room. Seconds later, she found her gaze drawn back to the man with the espresso. He looked interesting, intelligent. As he studied his paper, his brows were drawn together in concentration. Who was he? What was he doing here in this Laura Ashley nightmare of a place? Would it be terribly unsubtle to go and sit at the table next to him? There were about nine other tables in the shop but she decided what the hell, she would sit there. He was so engrossed in his paper that he probably wouldn't have noticed if she sat on his lap.

But he did notice when Clare spilled her coffee there instead.

She flew into a panic, blushing furiously, apologising and dabbing at his pale blue shirt with a paper napkin. Suddenly he grabbed her wrist, to stop her frantic fussing. Their eyes met and for a moment she couldn't tell what he was thinking at all. His eyes were of such a dark brown that you could hardly see where the irises ended and his pupils began. They were expressionless for what seemed like an age, then they began to crinkle at the corners and what could have turned into a snarl became a smile.

'Stop fussing,' he told Clare in a low, quiet voice. 'It was my fault since it was my case that you tripped over . . . This shirt could do with a wash anyway, and it was your coffee that was spilt. Sit down and I'll buy you another one.'

Clare sat down next to him in a daze and he clicked his fingers to summon the attention of the girl behind the counter who practically flew across the room to do his bidding. As the waitress neared, he took off his coffee-stained shirt, since the quickly cooling wet patch was making him uncomfortable, and revealed a tight sleeveless vest. The woman who owned the café tutted in disapproval.

'Do you think they have a dress code here?' the man laughed.

Clare's eyes met those of the girl who was taking their order over a well defined bicep. She raised her eyebrows and smiled conspiratorially.

He was indeed something to raise your eyebrows about. Though slightly older than Clare had first imagined when viewing him from the back, he obviously took very good care of himself. The muscular arms, which were now folded on the gingham tablecloth, were matched by a pair of equally muscular legs in close-fitting blue jeans. His hair was just long enough to be sexily unkempt. The fringe flopped into his eyes from time to time to be pushed away by light tan fingers with beautifully manicured nails. His eyes were extraordinary, and Clare was surprised to get the feeling, which she had found in the past rarely to be wrong, that it wouldn't be too long before she saw them closed in ecstasy. She found herself wishing that she had gone to get her hair done before having lunch as she casually laid her left hand over a paint stain on her right sleeve.

His name was Steve. He was in property, he told her, in St Ives overseeing the conversion of a few big places into little holiday flats before the next season began. Home for him was normally London so they found common ground there, talking about the pollution, the traffic, the stress. And blood pressure. Clare's, at that particular moment, seemed much higher than usual.

Clare said that she was an artist and he seemed genuinely interested when she told him about her artistic ambitions, even nodding knowledgeably when she mentioned a couple of the painters she emulated – names which normally drew nothing more than a blank look. He asked where she was living and she told him but when he asked who with she found herself saying 'just a friend'. As soon as she had said that she lowered her eyes as if he would be able to look into them at that moment and see the lie. Clare swirled what was left of her coffee around in the cup. She had picked nervously at the pasta salad and couldn't even start the shortcake.

'You've got a little way to walk to get home,' he said, when they had both finished. 'I think I may be going that way. Can I give you a lift?'

Clare said yes. The eyes of the women behind the counter seemed to be burning into her back as they left, but what the hell? She was only accepting a lift after all and he was such an interesting guy, she wanted to talk to him for just a little longer.

Clare tried not to look too pleased when she saw his car. A sleek racing green sports model, upholstered in creamy leather stood with its top down in the tiny car-park. He opened her door and she slipped inside.

'Nice car,' Clare breathed. Thinking to herself, 'I could get used to this.'

'Looks even better now,' he replied, smiling at Clare's legs as her long wrap-around skirt took that opportunity to get caught in the door and pull open.

'What make is it?' Clare asked, running her fingers along the dashboard, and making it clear with her eyes that she'd like to be running her fingers across Steve.

'It's a TVR Griffith,' he told her as he started up the powerful engine. 'But I call it Frankie.'

'Frankie?'

'Long story.'

Steve began to drive and Clare felt guiltily disappointed that he headed straight back to her place and didn't attempt to spin the journey out. She got him to drop her on the corner of the road where she lived. The last thing she needed was for grouchy Daniel to see her getting out of some green mean machine, so she told Steve that it would be easier for him to stop there. As they said goodbye there was an awkward moment between them. Clare contemplated asking him in for a coffee, sure that Daniel would enjoy talking to this guy as well, but something prevented her. The promise of something other than a friendship in the way he kissed her hand in farewell.

'Well, it was lovely to talk to you,' he told her.

She nodded.

'I'll see you around, I hope,' he said.

'Maybe,' Clare replied.

She watched as he drove off. The nervous tingle which had been with her at the café had still not abated. Neither had the disappointment that he hadn't taken the opportunity to whisk her straight off to some deserted hill-top car-park, but, as she stepped out of the car, Clare had noticed a familiar little white envelope, out of which poked a gold-embossed invitation. It had been tucked down the side of the passenger seat. Perhaps she would be going to the party at the Dragon Gallery after all . . .

# Chapter Three

'**DO YOU WANT** to come to Graham's party?'
Clare asked Daniel as she slicked on another layer
of deep plummy lipstick. 'I feel that I've got to go
because Graham has been so good about taking
my paintings but it'll just be full of people from
the art society talking about their children's piano
lessons and mortgages and . . .' Daniel was
already shaking his head. A thrill of excitement
raced through her. She was going to the party on
her own.

'You look very pretty,' Daniel said as he
wandered into the bedroom. Clare smiled her
thanks, feeling a little guilty over the effort she
had been making. But she didn't have anything to
feel guilty about, she reminded herself . . . yet.

'Shall I help you do that up?' Daniel began to
button up the back of Clare's long red silk dress. It
was stunning, but not in an obvious way, clinging
tightly to the contours of her breasts and her
waist before flaring gently out in a sweep of fabric
that reached her ankles. She felt covered and

yet revealed. The feeling of the silk around her legs as she walked was like the caress of soft hands. Daniel fastened the last button and then ran his hands down the line of her body in appreciation, giving a low whistle as he did so.

'Do you think I should wear my hair up?' Clare asked. 'With this dress?'

'I don't know,' said Daniel, smiling. 'I can't have you going out looking too beautiful.'

Clare began to pin her long, gently waving hair up away from her neck.

'Ah well,' Daniel sighed, stroking a finger lazily up her exposed nape. 'I suppose I'll just have to hope you're going to let me help you take all this off later on.' Clare kissed him on the tip of his nose, leaving a bright ring of lipstick there.

As Clare walked through the town, down the steeply sloping streets to the Gallery in the chilly night air, she found herself humming an old tune she always used to play on her stereo when she and her best friend, Anna, were sixth formers, getting ready to go out and do some under-age drinking in one of their grotty home town pubs. They would have been planning their Saturday night all week. Even co-ordinating their outfits so that they complimented each other and didn't clash. They would start putting their make-up on at five in the afternoon! But that was part of the fun. Saturday nights were always full of promise, the air heavy with hairspray and expectation. Whether chatting up someone gorgeous or putting down someone grotesque, they always had a brilliant time. Walking to the Gallery, she felt that Saturday feeling. How she'd missed it, going out with Anna and the other girls. At college, the social scene had been all couples. Clare wanted a bit of flirtation again . . . seduction.

She would give Anna a ring the very next day. See if she wanted to come down for a weekend. Clare could ship Daniel off to one of his mates in London and she and Anna could relive the wild time they had had in Cornwall after finishing their A Levels. They had spent a week in Newquay, while the Hot Tuna Surf Championships were taking place. The weather had been great; they sat on the beach all day and in some pub or other all night. They'd scored left, right and centre. In fact, Anna had managed to pull a really great guy who turned out to live just nine miles away from their home town. They were still together. They had a mortgage now. In fact, getting Anna to leave her Ikea-clad pad and come to Cornwall for a wild weekend would probably be just marginally easier than squeezing blood from a stone these days. Clare stopped just in view of the Gallery and looked up at the stars. Was that what she and Daniel had in store now that they had left college and were officially living together? Better furniture and less sex?

The face of the man she had met in the café slipped in amongst her memories and she found herself smiling in anticipation of seeing him again. Nothing would come of it, she told herself, but it would be nice to flirt. Nice to have someone new and different appreciate the way she looked. See her first and foremost as a woman, rather than as an artistic rival and an unpaid maid, which was how she felt Daniel sometimes saw her these days, and not necessarily even in that order. A street away from the Gallery she stopped and checked her lipstick in the wing mirror of a car. No smudges, still a perfect outline. Kissable, she thought, just kissable.

Graham smiled warmly as usual when Clare walked through the door into his party, but his face positively rivalled the Blackpool illuminations when he realised that she had no boyfriend in tow.

'Lovely to see you,' he trilled, wrapping an arm around her silk-clad waist and ushering her into the main room. 'Where's your boyfriend?' he asked, as if he really wanted to know.

'Where all good men should be. He's chained to my bed,' Clare winked and thought that Graham might even have blushed.

Graham made a few quick introductions which she didn't really take in. She was surprised to see that so many guests had already arrived. She scanned the room hopefully, nodding hellos to familiar faces, but she was disappointed to see no trace of Steve. Perhaps he was in the adjoining room, from which people were emerging with glasses of champagne and punch. As soon as it was humanly and politely possible, Clare would excuse herself from the little group of aspiring watercolourists to whom she had just been introduced, and head for that room. Her pulse quickened a little at the thought that Steve could be just behind that door.

27

'A drink, Clare?' Graham asked. 'Champagne? Punch?'

'Yes,' she said eagerly, 'but don't worry about me, I'll get it.'

Clare made a dash for the other room. Of course Steve wasn't inside. She glanced at her watch. It was quarter past eight. The party had only started at half past seven. He was the kind of person who would probably turn up to one of these dos later rather than as soon as the door opened. But how much later? She'd been at the party for five minutes and had already exhausted all the conversation she had for any of the other guests. It crossed her mind more and more frequently that he might not even come at all. Just because he had an invitation . . . After all, before Clare had seen his invitation and thought that he might be at the party, she had been going to try and give this evening with Graham a miss.

Clare wondered how Steve knew Graham.

'Clare, Clare,' Graham was calling, 'There's someone here I'd like you to meet.' Steve perhaps? She poured herself a glass of the champagne punch, in which rose petals floated for extra effect, and strolled back into the main room, smoothing down her hair and plastering on her best smile.

'Clare, meet Henry.'

Clare struggled to keep the warm smile on her face as a tall, thirty-something guy with a floppy fringe held out his hand to her. His hand-shake was as limp as his hair and once the formalities of introduction were over, he just stood there in front of Clare, saying nothing, watching her avidly as if the true meaning of life was about to come from her lips. Graham had disappeared to circulate. He must have introduced me to Henry deliberately, Clare thought – a ploy to make her so desperate by the end of the evening that Graham's limited charms would be as irresistible as Harrison Ford's.

'I need the loo,' Clare told her new acquaintance, two minutes later, when she had finished her potted autobiography and he still showed no sign of starting his own. Henry nodded enthusiastically. Clare sloped off with the intention of spending fifteen minutes reapplying her lipstick before she slipped back into the room and made a bee-line for the corner opposite the one in which Henry was lurking. When she emerged twenty minutes later there was still no sign of Steve. How long should she give him? How long could she stand to give him, more to the point? Henry was scanning the crowd as well . . . for Clare. It was unbelievable to her that there should be a man in the room she wanted to be with even less than Graham.

'Graham, Graham!' Clare called, as Henry finally got her in his sights. Graham was wandering past with a couple of glasses of punch for his guests. When he had delivered them, he shot straight back to Clare and wrapped his arm around her waist again.

'Having a good time?' he asked.

'Oh, yes,' she smiled graciously, it was almost as good as her sixteenth birthday party, when Susie Powell had turned up in exactly the same dress and scored with Clare's boyfriend, who claimed that he was drunk and confused. 'But please rescue me from that dreadful man . . .' Graham was only too pleased, and immensely flattered.

It was half past ten. Steve still hadn't turned up. As Clare sipped a third glass of champagne punch – she'd been taking it slowly, because if Steve wasn't going to turn up, she certainly didn't want to be at the mercy of Graham – she wondered how she could make her escape. Graham was showing a couple of insipid prints to the wife of a local councillor. While he was so engrossed, Clare could just slip out of the door. It would be a little rude not to say goodbye but every time she had tried to say goodbye so far that evening, he had introduced her to another local art world bigwig and she'd been forced to prolong her stay. What a great night, she thought sarcastically. She was feeling slightly less spectacular in her red silk dress now. Some idiot had managed to spill punch down her back.

The councillor's wife had dragged Graham on to explain another painting that was further still from the door. Slowly, Clare crept backwards, like a child playing a game, not turning round until the last moment so that, should Graham look towards her, it wouldn't look as if she was making a bid for freedom at all. It was while she was walking backwards, not looking where she was going, that she crashed straight into a familiar back, sending a drink swirling through the air in an arc, to land, once again, on an expensive clean shirt.

'Oh my goodness,' Clare exclaimed in delight as she joyfully recognised her victim. 'Steve, I am so sorry.'

'You again,' he smiled, his face mirroring the pleasure on hers. 'I might have known. Where were you going, walking backwards like that?'

'I was making my escape,' she muttered sheepishly.

'Good idea.'

'You been here long?'

'Ten minutes or so.'

'I've been here since eight.'

They laughed conspiratorially. Graham looked over when he heard the sound of their laughter over the quiet hum of conversation.

'Look serious,' Steve told Clare. 'The last thing we want is for Graham to think we're having a good time and come over to join us.' Clare pulled a mock grave face.

Graham returned to his deep discussion with the councillor's wife.

'I really think I'm going to have to go now, Steve, before I become one of the permanent exhibits,' Clare told him. She was acting casual as she tried to put the idea of joining her into his mind.

'Are you heading home or heading on?' he asked. 'Can I join you?'

It had worked. Easy! 'I suppose so,' Clare shrugged. 'We could go for a walk on the beach.'

'I could certainly use the air. Right –' Steve grabbed her arm – 'We'll walk backwards towards the front of the Gallery, I'll start to push the door open and when I say go, we'll leg it.'

31

Clare nodded, and they began their retreat. 'Go,' Steve hissed when Graham's back was safely turned. They tumbled out into the car-park, giggling like children. 'Quick, let's get into the car!' Frankie the TVR was waiting, this time with its top up. Clare clambered inside and they sped off, tyres spinning in the gravel, just as Graham appeared at the gallery door, to bid another, more polite guest goodbye.

'He'll be so offended,' Clare said, looking out of the back window at the shrinking figure of their host.

'He'll get over it.'

'How do you know him, the gorgeous Graham?'

'Gorgeous? Surely you mean "gargoyle".' Steve laughed. He hesitated momentarily before he told her, 'I met him about five years ago, through a friend . . .' Clare didn't notice the way his voice tailed off.

'Some friend,' she smiled.

Steve pushed a compact disc into the player and suddenly the car was filled with the strains of stringed instruments and a girl singing about lost love.

'Where to?' he asked.

'Surprise me,' Clare replied, surprising herself. This time Steve wasn't going to be driving her straight home. She glanced at her watch and wondered how long she could risk staying out before Daniel started to worry, then, satisfied she had a couple of hours, she settled back into the deep, leather seat and gazed out of the window at the passing scene, then gazed inside the car at the profile of its driver. So beautiful. Better than she remembered. He had such a powerful profile. His lips were parted as he murmured along with the song.

Steve turned to smile at her. He slipped the car into fourth then his hand left the gear lever and alighted gently on her silk-covered knee. His eyes checked for a positive reaction while Clare felt almost breathless with the realisation that, if she wanted it, then this was it. Her cheeks prickled with heat as the exploratory hand began to move up her thigh.

'My hotel?' he asked quietly.

Clare took a deep breath and nodded her assent. His hand squeezed her thigh tighter in approval.

'Every woman deserves a sexual adventure,' Clare reminded herself as she watched the lights of the Gallery get smaller and smaller until they were gone.

# Chapter Four

WHEN CLARE GOT back to the flat in the early hours of the morning, Daniel was already in bed. When he asked where she had been she told him that she had stayed behind, with a few of the others, to help clear up after the party. Then, she continued, they all went back to Graham's house for a night-cap. Clare claimed that a girl Daniel didn't know had given her a lift home. He didn't question her any further.

'Come to bed,' he murmured, stretching an arm out from beneath the duvet.

Clare shook her head. 'I want to get some painting done while I'm still in the mood,' she told him. 'Graham wants some more boat pics for the weekend.'

'But it's the middle of the night!' Daniel exclaimed. 'And I've been waiting and waiting for you to come back so that I could help you off with that dress . . .'

A guilty shudder ran through her but Clare gaily shrugged her shoulders as she reminded him, 'You can't choose when you're going to get hit with a flash of inspiration.'

'See if I care,' he grunted.

Yes, things had been getting a bit 'like that' between them lately, blowing hot and cold depending on whether or not Daniel felt he was getting his own way.

Clare wandered into their 'studio'. A canvas that Daniel had obviously cut up in anger while Clare was at the party was in bits all over the place. Any other night it might have bothered her, but not that night. She kicked some of the larger pieces of debris into a corner and set her own work up. She had a wonderful piece of canvas, larger than she usually used for the tourist paintings, which she had kept in reserve for the moment when that fickle muse struck. He had struck that afternoon in the café and again, tonight, at Graham's party. As Clare picked up her brush to make the first few marks she remembered the first touch of Steve's hand around her wrist. The wave of fear and excitement that had washed through and over her as she looked for the first time into those fascinating eyes. The evil anticipation of what she knew she was inviting when he asked her who she lived with and she told him 'just a friend'. And the illicit thrill of accepting a lift from a party, with a virtual stranger, after dark, that Clare knew would take her nowhere near home.

Her brush traced the outline of a strongly muscled shoulder.

They had skipped a late-night drink at the hotel

bar and tripped stealthily through the quiet corridors to Steve's room that overlooked the churning sea. Outside a light wind was whipping up tiny waves that speckled the blackness of the sea with white when the moon shone through a gap in the clouds. Standing by the window, looking out at the white horses and the reflection of the moon on the sea, Clare had shivered and Steve had put his arm around her, to keep her warm. Her skin was electrified as his fingers closed around her narrow shoulders.

His lips traced a path from the lobe of her ear to her shoulder. Instinctively, Clare turned around so that she was facing him, her forehead level with his lips. He took her chin in his hand and tilted her head back a little so that he was looking into her eyes. From deep within her, Clare felt the first ripple of anticipation, spreading out below her waist and up to her neck, making her nipples harden slowly so that when he asked her to lift her arms and carefully pulled her dress up over her head without unbuttoning it, they were already poking suggestively forward through her thin camisole. If Clare's mind was having doubts about the seduction of an impossibly handsome stranger in a hotel room, it was obvious that her body had already made its decision.

Steve ran two curious hands over the outline of Clare's cream silk-clad torso, his thumbs gently brushing across the unfaithful pink tips of her nipples. He leant forward to kiss her on the lips, softly, just once. It was hardly even a kiss at all, but the prelude to a kiss, before he quietly asked her to raise her arms again and discarded the camisole in the same direction as the dress.

A whisper of wind lifted the gauzy curtain from the window so that it brushed against Clare's back as Steve's lips brushed against the pale winter-white flesh of her belly. Clare shivered again, not with cold but delight. It was as if she was being seduced by a ghost and she wondered how long she would be able to stand these half-caresses before the wetness which was gathering between her legs made her beg him for something more.

It was as Steve knelt to explore her navel with his long probing tongue that Clare felt she could stand it no longer. She grabbed his golden brown head in her hands and pulled him up towards her lips. That tongue, at least, should be exploring the inside of her mouth.

As they kissed, hard, they staggered backwards towards the bed. Clare, almost naked. Steve, still fully clothed, though now slightly dishevelled. Clare scrabbled frantically with the buttons of his white shirt, with its red wine stain like a gunshot wound through his heart, and began to pull it away from his shoulders. He kissed her ever harder, squeezing her right breast with one hand as he used the other to pull down her smooth silk knickers. As soon as they were out of the way, he made just one quick circuit of the silky brown triangle of her pubic hair before returning, tantalisingly, to toy with both her breasts.

'Put something in me,' Clare pleaded. 'Something, anything!'

She felt she could drown in her own wetness. Never had she come so close to an orgasm while her clitoris remained so neglected. Steve continued to kiss her as if he had been starving for her mouth, but now, at last, his hand ventured lower.

There was no need for him to trace playfully around the lips of her vagina now. She was wet, open, ready. He slipped a finger straight inside and began to bring her to the point of no return with long, deliberate thrusts. The knuckle of his thumb, meanwhile, was hard against her clitoris, massaging hard in a way she had never before experienced. Clare's breathing was more shallow now, ragged, as each stroke took her by surprise.

The sensation was incredible. Unbearable!

Waves of tension flooded towards her vagina, building up like a sneeze that never, ever came. Clare couldn't come . . . or was she already coming? His thumb moved faster as the finger slid in and out, in and out, keeping the rhythm. The wave built up to her vagina again and spilled over . . . but not in the usual way. She could feel a shuddering gathering in her legs which made her want to draw them up to her chest and hug them until the feeling passed away.

'What are you doing?' Clare asked him breathlessly as she writhed on the silky sheet. The muscles in her stomach were contracting now, connected to the circuit. Waves of electricity were shooting up and down the side of her rib-cage, making goosebumps as they passed. Her hand instinctively flew down to where he was playing. If this next wave broke over the barrier she couldn't be held responsible for the number of innocents drowned!

'Stop,' Clare groaned, pushing his hand away

from her pulsing vagina. The intensity was just too much. But he was stronger, keeping his fingers in place while using his other hand to hold her own protesting one away. His finger advanced inside her again while his thumb continued its own game on her clit. The feelings he was producing were so intense that Clare wasn't sure whether he had a finger in her anus as well. From the waist down she was afire. 'No, Steve, please. Stop.' She writhed her body away from him and in doing so helped him drive his finger further in again.

'I have stopped,' he told her. A twitch at her G-spot said otherwise.

'Stop properly, take your hand away. I don't think I can stand it . . .' Her words were lost as she panted for breath.

'Do you really want me to?' he asked, his mouth touching hers as he whispered. She nodded, she couldn't say anything. 'I'm not moving my hand at all,' he continued. But Clare could still feel something, a pulsing deep inside her. 'It's you that's moving.' Then he commanded, 'Tighten your muscles around my finger.'

Clare did as she was told and the sensation was suddenly amplified. 'Again,' he whispered, 'Again.' The muscles of her vagina rippled, caressing his finger. She enjoyed it. She was beginning to enjoy it. She was in control. Her vagina was caressing his finger! And each time she contracted it was as if he was plunging it deeper into her!

'I'm not doing a thing,' Steve laughed. 'Do you still want me to stop?'

'No,' Clare squealed, as the barrier finally broke and she had to bite into his shoulder while her body rippled like a crazy concertina on the inside and the outside and she soaked the sheet with come.

'I think I just had my first multiple orgasm.'

It wasn't long before she was ready for her second.

Clare lay on her back looking up at Steve's concentrated face. Now he was kneeling between her legs and had finally slipped off his trousers and stripy shorts so that when she cast her gaze down his body, it met with the picture of the perfect penis. Thick and long and pointing straight back at her. And just above it, nestling where his thigh smoothly became his groin, a tattoo, a blue and green serpent. He saw her look at it, pleasantly surprised.

'I was eighteen,' he said. 'It was my nickname.'

'The serpent?'

'Well, Steve the Snake actually,' he blushed.

Laughing with him, Clare reached out to trace with her finger the little picture. His cock bobbed for attention.

'That tickles.' Steve shuddered as his words made her trace the snake again, this time with a nail.

'I bet you had it put there for exactly that reason,' Clare told him.

Less patient with teasing than she was, Steve took hold of Clare's wrist and guided her wandering hand to his cock, which was smooth and hot to her touch. She curled her fingers gently around its pleasantly full girth and slid her fisted fingers slowly down over the shaft, which was already sticky with its own emission. Clare slid her hand down his cock just once and when she took her hand away it twitched convulsively upwards again, as if in indignation. Steve took her face in his hands again and kissed her full, blushing lips.

'Carry on,' he whispered.

Clare slicked her hand upwards again, gradually building up a rhythm. Beneath her fingers, she could feel him getting harder and harder. With her free hand she tickled his balls.

'Stop,' he said suddenly. 'I feel like I'm going to come.'

'Then come,' Clare replied.

'No, I want to do something different.' Quickly, Steve began to roll on a condom, his face concentrated into a frown. Clare continued to tickle his balls to remind him she was still there. Within seconds the condom was on and he slid himself down again so that he was supported now on his arms, his legs between her shivering white thighs.

'Are you sure you want to do this now?' he asked gravely.

Clare had never been more sure of what she wanted in her life. She kissed his lips in reply, pulling him closer to her with one arm around his neck as her other hand slid down between them to guide him in between her longing lips. Her legs trembled in anticipation of this moment. As she touched her inner thighs in passing she noticed that they were still damp from the climax he had just made her give herself with his hand.

Steve's penis hovered temptingly at the lips of

Clare's vagina. He moved himself up and down slowly, just grazing her lips as she scrabbled to take hold and bring his penis home.

'Let's do this slowly,' he purred, as the first, joyful inch slipped in and was withdrawn.

'Don't tease me,' Clare hissed.

'I never tease,' he lied, teasing her again with another shallow dive. And another and another. Just enough to make her sigh with disappointment as she felt all too short a length being withdrawn.

'I can't stand this.'

'Do you want me to stop?'

'No, no, I don't.' For a second he was hovering around the edge of her vagina again, then she took his buttocks in both her hands and lifted her thighs, pulled him right into her, and drove his penis home. Now she sighed with ecstasy and the pumping could begin in earnest, his energy driving her down into the soft white sheets while she clutched him to her and drew her fingernails up his back. Her heart was pounding so hard that she was sure that he could feel it too, pumping through her flesh and through his. She tried to keep her eyes open and focused on the face that loomed above her. His eyes were closed, his mouth open as he breathed more and more heavily as the movements of his pelvis became faster, more urgent. Clare suddenly lifted her trembling legs from the bed and wrapped them around his slim waist. She pulled his cock deeper inside with her muscles, squeezing as he had showed her before. 'Aaah!' the delicious extra pressure on his dick was bringing his climax too close now, he couldn't hold off any longer and his firm strokes began to lose their rhythm. Clare ground her pelvis against him, exerting as much pressure on her clitoris as she could in that position. She too was beginning to lose control. The moment had taken over and Clare's whole being was trying to pull him closer, closer, further into her body, until the spasms that she could no longer hold back forced him to empty his passion into her, his head jerking backwards with each jet he spurted inside her. Eyes screwed tightly shut, his face the perfect picture of the peculiar agony of sex.

Back in the studio, Clare stood back to take a good look at the painting she had been working on. The man stood with his back to her, but the shadow, the outline of Steve's body was unmistakable. The strength in the shoulders, sweeping down to the slim waist around which she had wrapped her arms as she had kissed and tongued his cock so greedily. Clare could almost smell him. The sensual smell of sweat, soap and sex. Smells of the sophisticated man and the primitive creature within him. The taste of salt as she licked a line from the base of his balls to the tip of his penis where a silvery drop of semen had gathered in anticipation of the arrival of her lips at his most sensitive part.

Clare had wrapped both hands around it, holding it like a bottle of water, precious after a long, dry walk across the desert. He had moaned as she let her tongue touch just that drop of semen, tasting it, savouring it. Just the tip of her tongue had reached out again and again to him, tantalising the delicate ridge as her hands carefully roamed over his balls. In a moment of mischief she had blown on to them, making them contract and stir in the coolness.

Clare's own hand now traced the line down her body that Steve had followed with his hands. Slowly, she unfastened her dress and slipped her hand inside. She wasn't wearing her camisole. In her haste to leave the hotel and get back to the flat, she had stuffed all her underwear into the voluminous pockets of her baggy jacket. So now, her fingers touched achingly bare flesh, a nipple already hardened and sensitised by the silk of her dress that had been rubbing against her breasts as she painted. Clare rolled her nipple between her fingers exactly as Steve had done, then she moved her attention to the other. She didn't want any part of her body to feel left out . . .

Suddenly Clare was aware of someone standing behind her. She turned around slowly. Daniel had got himself out of bed and was leaning against the door frame, silhouetted by the light in the kitchen. He was holding two glasses, clinking with ice, as he stepped tentatively across the room, avoiding the debris of his own canvas.

# Chapter Five

'THOUGHT YOU MIGHT be thirsty,' Daniel said, handing Clare a vodka on the rocks. He looked as if he had been crying.

'What did you paint?' he asked. Clare had thrown a sheet over the wet canvas at his approach.

'Nothing good. It went wrong,' she told him. He was almost lifting up the corner of the sheet. 'Don't look at it,' she implored him softly. 'You know I hate letting you see stuff that I'm not happy with.'

'I'm sure I would be impressed,' he assured her but he let the paint-splashed sheet drop again. The next day, Clare decided, she would have to get rid of her latest masterpiece.

'I'm sorry about earlier,' Daniel told Clare as he stood with his back to her, surveying the mess of his own ruined painting.

'No worries. It was my fault too. The fickle muse, eh?' Clare replied, knowing that his temper tantrum should be far outweighed in the guilt stakes by what she had just found herself doing. 'Let's go into the other room.' Even covered by a sheet, the portrait of the lover she had just painted burned into her mind, and her clitoris still pulsed gently in anticipation of a favourable climax to the self-pleasure she had just begun to give.

Now Clare felt strangely shy of this man she had known for so long. She sat on the sofa with the glass in her hands, swirling the liquid around nervously, avoiding Daniel's eyes as they talked about mundane things. What they had been doing that week. The football. Could he tell, she wondered. Did she look different? Did she smell different? She had only had time for a very quick shower before leaving the hotel, telling Steve that she had to go home because her housemate was returning from London at about five in the morning and had forgotten to take his key.

Daniel was perching on the coffee table opposite Clare on the sofa. He had opened his legs so that her knees were caught between his. Suddenly, as she was looking to the honey-coloured floorboards again, racking her brain for some sporting event to discuss, he took the glass from her hands and raised her fingers to his lips. His mouth trailed across them, one after the other, and then, drawing Clare closer, his lips touched her lips and they broke the ice that had formed between them with a kiss.

A tender touch for just a moment and then they began in earnest. His tongue forced her lips apart. Clare opened her mouth wider to let him probe inside. He traced her teeth with the quivering tip.

His tongue was penetrating her, echoing the actions he longed to make with other parts of his body. His hand on the back of her head, first gently guiding and then bringing her firmly towards him. A handful of her hair grasped in his fist. Causing Clare no pain but giving such a wonderful impression of force. Clare was melting into him.

Then, suddenly, a cold slash of sensation across her leg. They were sliding together, from the sofa to the floor and on their lustful journey had knocked Clare's half full glass over with them. Clare's body shuddered, but she was grateful for something so cool in the midst of all the heat that they were generating.

Now they writhed on the floor in a puddle of ice. Daniel clutched up a handful of it, eager not to waste any sensation. The top of Clare's dress was rolled down out of the way and he made straight for her nipples. Tracing delicately around the hardening, rose-pink tips until the ice was barely big enough to hold anymore and instead he massaged one breast fully in each cold palm while the slivers of ice became cold water that mingled with her sweat. Clare's back arched upwards, pushing out her firm breasts for more, searching for Daniel's lips and tongue. But he was sitting back on his heels again.

'One left,' he announced. A solitary ice-cube had not escaped the glass which now lay on its side. Daniel picked it out and held it tantalisingly between thumb and forefinger. 'Where do you want it?'

Where did Clare want it? Where didn't she want it?

'You know where.'

A smile flickered across his long-lashed eyes as he lifted the hem of Clare's skirt and dropped his hand to her mons, which was already thrusting up to meet him halfway. Now he was tracing again, but this time across the lips of her sex, still burning with the passion of her liaison in the hotel. She felt sure that Daniel would notice, that they must be glowing red, but he had restoked the fire which had yet to die down properly and Clare suddenly didn't care. The ice-cube salved them for a moment. Melting water trickled gently down between them.

'Does that feel good?' Daniel asked, as he watched the expression on her face change. Her mouth opened slowly in a silent gasp of pleasure.

'Yeeeesss!' Clare shivered. The sensation was incredible. The ice-cold water felt like liquid gold to her.

'But you must be feeling very cold now,' Daniel continued. 'I think you need something to warm you up.'

While Daniel had been turning ice-cubes to steam on Clare's body, she had been struggling to rid him of the boxer shorts he had been wearing when he went to bed. Now he had given up resistance and she could already feel the tip of his penis nudging at her opening as he licked the salt of sweat from the edge of her mouth. The nudging became more insistent, and her lips began to be forced inwards as Daniel fought to make his way in. Clare went to help him with her hands.

'No don't,' he said. 'Enjoy the friction.'

Just two more pushes and he was in. Clare inhaled sharply at the first delicious full thrust.

'You . . . feel . . . so . . . good,' he told her. A word for each time he entered her. He placed a hand beneath the small of her back to protect her from the hard floor and to lift her pelvis higher so that he could drive deeper. She pushed down through her legs to help him on.

'Deeper, deeper,' Clare moaned, wanting more and more of him inside her still. His balls tapped against her perineum, intensifying the sensation, and her fingernails dug into the firm, twin cheeks of his bum as they tensed and relaxed, tensed and relaxed. Each time he plunged into Clare, he let out a small, animal-like grunt of pleasure, which transferred that pleasure to her. They became faster and faster, a grunt for each thrust, a thrust for each beat of her heart until, suddenly, the rapid thrusts became one long plunge. Daniel held himself in position against Clare's body, raised on his arms, his head thrown back, his mouth open, gasping for air, as his loins jerked convulsively.

Clare pushed up against him, willing his climax to continue forever as he flooded her with hot sticky come.

Afterwards, as they lay together on the rug, Clare couldn't stop a smile from passing across her lips. Daniel kissed it, thinking he had made her happy. But as Clare dreamily watched a spider walking across the ceiling, she was already thinking about the next time she could engineer a meeting with Steve.

Later Clare would ask herself why she didn't just throw that painting away. Things could have been so different. But when she woke up the morning after painting it and saw that Daniel was, thank goodness, still smiling, she figured that her soul probably hadn't been laid as bare by those brush strokes as she thought.

Graham at the Dragon Gallery raised an eyebrow as he eagerly tore away the brown paper in which Clare had wrapped the painting for the journey. He was expecting boats, not a butt. He held it at arm's length and turned it around and around, looking for the right way up, which, Clare supposed, wasn't entirely obvious.

'Is that your Daniel?' he asked.

'No, it's a fantasy work. Your party really fired my imagination.'

'What's it called?'

'It's called Graham. It's based on the way I imagine you must look beneath that mild-mannered maroon number.' Clare's liaison with Steve must have also fired her with a need for danger. She was actually flirting with Graham.

'Well, yes,' he blushed. 'I don't know if I'll be able to sell this one. It's very . . . er . . . erotic.' He turned it around again to catch the composition from another angle. 'But I guess I'll hang it. Since you named it after me.'

'So you enjoyed the party?' he asked as Clare watched the dark, brooding canvas take its place on the wall above a pastel portrait of a fisherman she had done a few weeks earlier. Clare nodded. 'I didn't see you leave,' Graham continued, 'Did you manage to get home all right? I was going to offer you a lift.' She nodded vacantly again. He wasn't going to draw anything out of her. 'Well, good. I don't like the thought of a girl going home on her own. You've got to be careful around some guys these days . . .'

Clare wasn't taking much notice. She was still gazing at the picture. It made her smile. Steve had touched something more in Clare than her G-spot. She was painting again. Really painting.

She was inspired.

'I think the American woman I told you about really liked the style of your landscapes . . . Keep them tasteful, eh?' Graham looked curiously at the girl's strange expression. 'Are you going to be able to get those done?'

'Mmm?'

'I said, are you going to be able to get those landscapes done for me?'

'What? Oh, yeah,' Clare suddenly refocused on Graham. 'Yeah. I feel like I could paint the Sistine Chapel today.'

'Really?' said Graham.

Clare tripped happily out of the gallery and went straight to the café where she and Steve had first met. She ordered exactly the same meal as she had that fateful day, for luck. She waited from twelve until two . . . but Steve didn't come.

Clare told herself that it was probably for the best. And anyway, if she grinned much more her face might have fallen in half.

# Chapter Six

'GET THE DOOR would you, Clare?' Daniel screamed. Clare was painting in the studio, he was painting at their bedroom window, finally deigning to take some inspiration from the quaint little houses which spread out below. The doorbell chimed again. Clare and Daniel were engaged in a battle over whose work was less important, who could afford to put down their brush on the off-chance that it wasn't the Jehovah's Witnesses. Clare lost.

Clare opened the door to a petite blonde, about her age, but considerably better dressed, in a pastel blue suit. She offered Clare a hand which wore two subtly expensive rings and smiled to show a row of equally expensively cared-for teeth. Clare wiped her hand, complete with bitten nails, clean on the seat of her jeans and they shook.

'Clare?' she asked.

The dark-haired girl nodded.

'I'm Francesca Philip. I saw your paintings in

the Dragon Gallery. I do hope you don't mind my coming here. I'd like to commission you to do a painting for me. Graham gave me your address. I hope I'm not disturbing you.'

'Of course not,' Clare smiled, then she realised that her visitor was still standing on the doorstep. 'Come in.'

Daniel was standing at the door to the studio, eager to see who was coming in. Clare gave him a stern look as she saw his eyes light up at the entrance of the petite blonde. The petite blonde who didn't seem to notice him standing there.

'What an unusual place you have here,' Francesca said as Clare made coffee. She perched on the edge of the sofa, too shy or polite to move out of the way the books and brushes that cluttered it. While the kettle boiled, Clare made a quick search of the lounge for a reasonably intact and unstained mug, since all those left in the kitchen were missing handles or other vital chunks. A pair of knickers, discarded several nights before, lay by the side of the sofa. Clare swiftly kicked them beneath it before Francesca had time to notice the extent of her bohemian slobbery.

'What kind of thing are you looking for? Boats a speciality,' Clare joked.

'No,' Francesca said, missing the joke. 'Your boat pictures were very nice but I was hoping for something more along the lines of your portrait. The one called "Graham". I must say I didn't realise that he was such a dark horse . . . It was a very sexy picture.'

Clare almost spluttered out the gulp of coffee

she had in her mouth. Just the memory of that particular canvas made her prickle with a blush but the thought that Francesca believed Graham had been the model was enough to make Clare really choke.

'What I want,' Francesca continued, 'is a special present for my husband. He's going to be forty in three weeks.'

A sugar-daddy, Clare laughed to herself.

'I think he'd like to have his portrait painted. I've got some photos that you can work from.' Francesca pushed an envelope towards Clare across the coffee table. Clare pushed a mug of coffee back towards her. 'I'll pay the going rate.'

As Clare opened the envelope, she played a game with herself. Trying to imagine what Francesca's husband would look like. Forty years old, knocking about with a girl at least fifteen years his junior who looked as though her hair was made of candyfloss. Fat, balding. Successful but short. Showering her with gifts as long as she was prepared to put up with him dressing up like a baby in bed.

'It should be quite an easy job since he's rather more symmetrical than Graham. He's very handsome, in fact,' Francesca assured the artist.

Clare nodded indulgently as she pulled out the first photo. The printed side was away from her. Clare turned it over and her jaw dropped. 'Don't you think so?'

It was Steve. The woman's husband was Steve. Unmistakable.

Trying not to get too frantic about it, Clare pulled the other photos out of the envelope.

There he was in the shirt she had spilled coffee down! And again, in front of an ivy-clad house, sitting on the bonnet of the very car in which he had driven Clare to the hotel where they had made love.

Frankie the car!

'What do you think? Are the photos clear enough? Do you think you can do it?' Francesca fired questions one after another.

Didn't she realise that Clare had already done it? Francesca had been attracted to Clare's work by her mind's eye portrait of Steve. Hadn't Francesca recognised him? Clare was beginning to be swallowed up by the horrible feeling of breathlessness that creeps up in the shadow of a shock. Her chest was tightening.

'Are you OK?' Francesca was leaning forward. She had laid her delicate hand on Clare's arm.

'Yes,' Clare told her. 'Yes, it's just the smell of the turps in here. Sometimes it makes me go a little faint. I really ought to get this room better ventilated.' Clare extricated herself from Francesca's concerned hold on her arm and swayed across to the window.

So it was Steve. So what? They'd met twice. Made love just once. No, you could hardly call it making love. They'd just had sex. Clare was living with a man she was supposed to love and Steve was married to some bimbo. It didn't matter. Clare struggled to compose herself. She needed the money she could get from this painting.

Clare took a few deep breaths of sea air while Francesca muttered something about the photos perhaps not being clear enough.

'No, no, they're clear enough. How do you want it done?' Clare asked, not listening as Francesca reeled off her requirements one by one.

'I'll need money for materials.' Francesca was already writing out the cheque – with the number Clare had thought of and another nought. She signed it and handed it over, grinning widely. The name at the bottom of the cheque swam before Clare's eyes. 'Mrs Francesca Philip.' Clare hadn't even known Steve's surname until then. She didn't know anything about him! But Steve the Snake suddenly seemed a very appropriate nickname indeed. 'Can I see it at various stages?' Francesca asked shyly.

'Yes,' Clare said. 'Of course.'

# Chapter Seven

AFTER FRANCESCA HAD gone Clare stood at the window for a long while, just looking out across the houses to the sea, thinking. That evening the sea was very calm. Just a few wispy, cotton-wool clouds crossed the pinky blue sunset and were echoed by the tiny white horses riding the waves. The beach was deserted but for a boy and his dog. The boy threw a stick and the dog barked, the distant noise carried up to the window by the wind so that it mingled with the calling of the gulls constantly wheeling overhead. The view from the flat where Clare and Daniel lived was almost the same as the view from Steve's hotel, though their flat was a little lower down the hill.

Steve, Steve, Steve. What had Clare been doing? She had never slept with a married man before and had always thought of the guys who had affairs as rats. In fact she had decided never to do the dirty on another girl right after the birthday party where Susie Powell stole her man and her pre-pubescent self-esteem. But at the same time, when Clare heard about people she knew and their affairs, she had also always assumed that the women these men cheated on must be doing something wrong. Not paying the guy enough attention. Letting themselves go in all the wrong ways. But Francesca? Francesca hadn't let herself go. She looked more like the kind of girl that wars were fought over, not a downtrodden wife. Bizarrely, Clare found herself recalling Francesca's face, and not her husband's.

Oh God, thought Clare, I should just forget it ever happened. He probably has.

Daniel had turned up the heating in the flat far too high and so the slight breeze which floated inland across the waves was welcome. As Clare leaned a little further over the ledge, the top of her navy crêpe wrap-around dress pulled open. She didn't do it back up but let the breeze play in over her breasts, caressing her nipples to stiffness. Why should she be bothered that Steve was married, she asked herself again. She was in love with Daniel. They had been going through a bit of a rough patch and she had wanted affection, well, not affection – action, passion. And the incident with the ice-cubes had proved that Daniel could still give her that!

A floorboard creaked in the room behind. 'Stay there,' Daniel told her. 'You look so beautiful.' He came nearer and soon he had slipped both his arms around Clare's waist. His chin rested on her shoulder as he too watched the soothing waves.

'Are you glad we're here and not in London?' he asked her.

The answer Daniel wanted wasn't totally clear

and so Clare gave the answer which was always in her mind when she looked out on to the sea instead of a railway track and a scrap yard. 'Yes,' she said. 'Of course I'm glad we're here.'

Daniel kissed her lightly on the cheek. 'Good. Well, I guess I ought to get back to work.' But the brief squeeze he gave her in parting couldn't help but become something more, an odyssey around the curves of her body. His lips hovered at the back of Clare's neck, while from her waist, his hands began to glide gently down over her hips. From the back to the front. He cupped one breast in each hand. First through the material of Clare's dress, then slipping his left hand inside to feel her skin.

'That's cold,' Clare exclaimed as her nipple leapt to attention.

'Sorry, I'll warm my hands up.' Daniel took his hands from her breasts and began to slide them down her body again, lingering at the curve of her waist. Soon he was at the hem of Clare's skirt, then under it. Sliding his hands back up her body on her bare legs. Clare stood still and silent as though none of this was happening, inwardly beginning to enjoy his gentle touch.

'This seems like a warm spot,' he whispered. Daniel's right hand had come to rest between her upper thighs, cupping her mound like the breast of a dove. Clare squeezed her thighs gently together in approval. His fingers carefully kneaded her for a moment or two. Then he was tugging at her white cotton panties, moving them out of the way before replacing his hand in that soft position. His fingers twisted a little of the silky dark hair.

Clare sighed. Daniel moved forward to kiss her

again on the back of the neck, his hand still between her legs. His fingers were moving somewhere else now. Tracing the line of her body from front to back. Teasingly skirting around her labia. Clare thrust her bottom backwards and up to help him find what he was looking for. As the first finger entered her vagina, Clare was already moist. But Daniel entered her so slowly, just a centimetre at a time. She found herself contracting each time he entered, trying to pull him further in.

'You hungry?' he quipped.

Clare laughed. She had had her eyes shut but now looked down on to the street below. A middle-aged couple ambled along, taking in the fresh evening air with their dog. Daniel suddenly thrust his finger a little harder, making Clare gasp out loud. The woman looked up at Clare's exclamation. She tried to retreat inside, but Daniel was hard behind her, blocking her escape.

'Daniel!' Clare hissed. Her right breast had earlier been freed by his hand. She tucked it back in hurriedly. 'There are some people walking past. They'll see.'

'They can't see below the level of the window-sill.'

Suddenly Daniel jammed Clare forward against the window-ledge with his hips. The couple were still passing, slowly. Daniel flicked up Clare's skirt so that it lay across her back, baring her ass to the room behind.

'Beautiful!' He kissed the pale smooth skin on each cheek. Then without further ado, he began unzipping the trousers, from which his hard-on had been planning its escape for a couple of minutes. He pressed his rigid shaft against her, making her giggle as he rubbed it up and down the cleft between her cheeks. Then, without speaking, Daniel parted Clare's lips and pushed the first inch inside. Though she was dripping with moisture at the thought of this first thrust, the friction still surprised her. Clare had to bite her finger in an attempt not to make any noise that would attract the attention of the people passing below. But as Daniel made a second thrust, so that his balls brushed right against her, pushing the air out from her lungs, Clare couldn't help but call out. The woman looked up again. Clare tried to dodge from her view but Daniel pushed her further forward over the ledge, and thrust and thrust.

'Stop it,' Clare hissed. 'Stop it now.'

'They can't see us,' Daniel told her as she tried to stop herself from popping in and out of the window like a demented cuckoo each time he entered and withdrew. With one hand Clare struggled desperately to keep her dress from falling away from her shoulders completely, while the other tried to stop her from flying straight out through the window. But it was clear that Daniel wasn't about to stop and soon one hand was joining in the fun, reaching back between her legs to stroke Daniel's balls, whenever his thrusting brought them bumping against her inner thighs.

'Are they still there?' he asked breathlessly.

'Yes!' Clare replied. The man was doing up his shoe as his wife tottered on. Clare could see him glance up surreptitiously and had to suppress the urge to wave.

'Are they looking?'

'The man is,' Clare panted.

'Good,' Daniel said. 'Give him a flash of your beautiful breasts.'

'Daniel!' Clare shrieked, half laughing. Whether she had decided to or not, the next thrust was so powerful that she had to use both her hands to stop herself from falling right over the ledge and into the old man's lap. Without her hand to keep her dress on her shoulders, she found that it promptly slipped off so that her breasts hung down like twin pink balloons.

She just had time to savour the astonished look that filled the man's eyes before Daniel pulled her inside to finish that fuck on the hard, shiny wooden floor. Still remaining inside her, he performed some kind of yoga move to grab a cushion from the settee and place it where the small of her back would be before he slammed Clare on to the boards, having managed to get from behind her to on top of her at the same time. Clare's stocking-clad feet were slipping on the varnished floor and, noticing this, he swiftly ripped the stockings off her legs, ruining them as he did so – not that she cared at the time. Before Clare knew what was happening, Daniel had used one of them to bind her hands together above her head, and then to bind her joined hands to the leg of the heavy dining table that sometimes served him as an easel.

Daniel slowly withdrew his prick and sat back on his heels to survey his handiwork. He unfastened the wrap-around dress so that her body was laid completely bare. With his strong hands on her parted thighs he pulled her so that her arms were stretched full length, giving him a better view of her chest, which was heaving with exertion and excitement.

'Mmm,' he smiled slowly. 'What am I going to do with you now?'

'Let me go, you b—' Before Clare could finish her sentence, Daniel had deftly tied the spare stocking around her mouth, preventing her protests. By the way her eyes were crinkling up at the corners he could tell that any protest was only for show anyway. Still holding on to her thighs, Daniel uncurled his legs and lay down on his front so that his mouth was level with Clare's sex. Her hips twisted away from him as his tongue made a first exploratory dip between her labia. Then he brushed her clitoris softly with his tongue.

'Nnnggh,' Clare grunted.

'I take it that means I can carry on?'

Daniel's tongue began to cover the length of Clare's now shiny vulva with hard, strong strokes. Her clitoris was achingly hard, her labia swollen and tingling. The strokes were slow at first, and made all the more pleasurable by the fact that Daniel's nose brushed against her clitoris as he licked. She closed her thighs tightly around his head to hold him there when the pleasure became particularly bad.

'Miss Nutcracker!' Daniel laughed as he unclamped her thighs from his ears and slid his body back up hers so that his lips were level with her gagged mouth. She could feel his penis nudging at her vagina again. Sliding in so easily between her lips soaked with desire.

'I want you to come with me,' Daniel was whispering in her ear as he moved his hips in and out. 'Come with me, Clare. Come with me now.' The strokes were getting faster. Urgent.

'Come, come, come,' he commanded her with each thrust.

Clare screwed her eyes tightly shut as the sensation continued to build within her.

'Come, come.'

Her inner muscles clamped hold of Daniel's dick as it reached for the entrance to her womb. She wanted to cry out loud, needed to scream something in ecstasy but the silken gag kept her silent.

'Come with me,' Daniel spoke in the voice of a body on the brink of delirium. His thrusting was uncoordinated now, his breathing taking on that familiar pattern. Clare's body tuned into his for the count-down, as she grunted in unison through her bondage.

'Come, come, aaaahhh!' An overhard thrust sent Clare knocking against the table as Daniel began to pump furiously into her body. Clare's open eyes saw a small pot of paint make a graceful arc through the sky to land with an indelicate plop on her chest as Daniel reared back from her body in orgasm.

It was too small to hurt but the hilarity of the moment somehow set Clare off and, while she laughed at the sensation of the red paint dribbling slowly across her breasts and beneath her armpits, her hips bucked with their own release.

Daniel withdrew, also laughing, and surveyed the damage. He untied the gag and kissed Clare's lips gently, getting smeared with red paint as their bodies touched. Then he sat back, still panting, and lazily traced a heart on her chest. He pierced it with an arrow and added the initials C & D.

# *Chapter Eight*

---

*CLARE STARTED WORK* on Steve's portrait the very next day. She chose to work from the picture of him sitting on his car outside the ivy-clad house, his family home. She chose it because he was wearing a forced, for-the-camera smile. It wasn't an expression Clare had seen on his face in the flesh and thus it was the nearest she could come to finding a picture which didn't remind her of his naked flesh every time she referred to it for her preliminary sketches.

After an hour or so Clare had produced a vague, compositional outline. She stood back and appraised her work. She felt no urge to slip her hand inside her blouse today. The picture wasn't working. It wasn't Steve. But so what? Francesca would think it was him, Francesca would see the jumper and the car and remember snapping the shutter on that strained smile and for her it would be Steven. Daniel wandered in and out of the studio with cups of coffee as Clare painted. He wasn't painting. He was having another off day.

'Mmm, nice jumper,' he said sarcastically as Clare started to add some colour.

'If only you knew,' she muttered.

'What?'

'I said, I need more blue,' Clare smiled.

Blues and greens. The painting was so cool. So different from Clare's much more passionate daub, made in the afterglow of love-making. Cool was how the Steven in the photos made Clare feel. Was this how he made Francesca feel? Detached. Indifferent. Cold? Or was it how he felt about her? A shiver of pride at her ability to have transformed the man into something altogether hotter ran through Clare. But what was going on in her life? The night before, when Daniel and Clare had made love by the window it was with the same intensity and passion as when they first made love years before. There was nothing wrong with that part of things.

Graham rang later that day to tell Clare that he had sold another three of her paintings. Clare wasn't in a hurry to get the money as Francesca's advance had been more than generous, but since Daniel was in one of his moods, mooching around the house like a storm just waiting to break, Clare felt as though she could use the walk. She didn't even look into the café where Steve had first appeared in her life but walked by quickly, breathing deeply to clear her lungs and her head.

Graham's wide smile failed to provoke any similar reaction from Clare's face.

'Hey, what's up, beautiful?' he asked, using her frown as an excuse to sling a fatherly arm around her shoulders. 'You look like you could do with a nice cup of tea and a chat with your old friend, Graham. Boyfriend troubles, eh?'

He sounded hopeful.

'Well, yeah,' Clare recalled the row she had with Daniel the night before, only hours after they had made love so passionately. His jealousy that her paintings sold while his didn't. His claim that she was growing distant, that while they still seemed to be making love all the time, she never initiated sex any more.

'Tell me all.'

'Oh no, Graham,' Clare said, recovering her composure and extricating herself from his tightening embrace. 'You really don't want to know.'

'But I do, I do . . .'

'It's probably just pre-menstrual tension.' Clare lied. There was nothing like the hint of 'women's problems' to make most guys of Graham's ilk cool right off. When Clare was assured that his bubble was safely burst, she accepted his offer of tea.

'Did my lovely young friend Francesca come and visit you?' Graham asked as he stirred three spoonfuls of sugar into his own cup. 'You're sweet enough aren't you?' he had said, when Clare declined sugar for her own.

'Yes, she turned up on Tuesday,' Clare told him. 'She wants me to do a painting for her of . . .'

'Her husband, Steve,' Graham picked up with the words Clare could hardly bring herself to say. 'Interesting chap, Steve, though far too good-looking for my liking. He was at the gallery party . . . briefly. Did I introduce you to him?' His eyes sought hers.

'No.' Clare stared at the steaming brown liquid in her cup.

'Funny, I thought I saw you two talking . . . Anyway, I don't know him that well. I only met him when he married Francesca – actually at their wedding in fact. Her elder brother was in my class at school . . . Yes, I remember Francesca when she had pigtails; we all teased her mercilessly about her frizzy hair and braces while she was growing up but when she hit eighteen – talk about the tale of the ugly duckling. We all fancied her, but Robert, her brother, wouldn't let us anywhere near. I guess he'd heard us all talking about the other girls we'd seen and didn't want her to be discussed in the pub as another notch on the bed-post. It wouldn't have been like that though . . .'

Graham's eyes looked into the past.

'Anyway, we were all horribly jealous of Steve,' he suddenly snapped back to the present and fixed his eyes on Clare's. 'And all Robert's fussing about not wanting any of us scumbags near her seemed a bit pointless when she went off and married a twice-married thirty-five-year-old anyway.'

'Steve had been married before?' Clare asked, realising even as she spoke the words that she was showing an inordinate amount of interest in the personal life of a man she was claiming never to have met.

But Graham was only too pleased to let her have the details. 'Yes, he was. Quite spectacularly, in fact. His first wife was that American singer, Laura Bollinger. I can't think of anything she actually sang, but she always seemed to be opening gold envelopes at award ceremonies. She was twenty years older than him and worth a fortune.' Graham rolled his eye to emphasise just how much of a fortune. 'He met her in the French Alps, at Chamonix, while she was learning to ski, apparently. He was her ski instructor.' Graham gave a little snort of disdain and took a slurp of his tea before carrying on. 'Ironically, it was on a skiing holiday two years later that she fell and broke her neck ... His second wife, American, affluent, and just twelve years his senior, had a swimming pool accident.' Graham added nonchalantly. 'Still, third time lucky eh?'

Clare nodded, hardly able to believe her ears. What was Graham suggesting? That Steve the Snake had a bite to match that of his namesake?

'So, now he's in town overseeing the development of a new holiday accommodation complex. That was Francesca's father's business; but he died earlier this year leaving the job unfinished. Robert, Francesca's brother, has emigrated to New Zealand – he met a nice Kiwi girl – so he couldn't take the project on. Steve was at a loose end, since his own business had just folded. Now, that was a strange affair ... But anyway, as I said, I only met Steve at his wedding, so I haven't really known him long enough to cast aspersions.'

Clare raised her eyebrows – what had he been doing thus far?

'It was a great wedding.' Clare was sure that he was placing emphasis on that word and then checking her eyes for a reaction. She smiled and nodded as if he were an auntie telling her about the price of cabbages. 'I was an usher,' Graham continued, 'and I nearly raised a "just impediment" when the vicar asked, but that's yet another story . . .'

Clare didn't press him to hear it. Something told her that a conversation about the wedding of Steve and Francesca Philip would be almost as unbearable for Graham as it was for her.

'Francesca is a very beautiful woman,' Clare said to close the subject.

Graham nodded. He was far away again.

# Chapter Nine

*FRANCESCA CAME TO* see how the painting was getting on just a couple of days after Clare started to paint it. Clare was alone in the flat, Daniel having driven back to London for a couple of days to try and persuade some galleries to display his work there. Francesca explained that her husband was in the area on family business, turning some houses into flats for the tourists. She could only come down to see him occasionally because she had a business of her own these days, a boutique in Chelsea.

Bought to keep her out of the way, Clare thought unkindly. She could imagine what it was like. Full of the kind of peachy pale clothes Francesca was wearing now, populated by bored housewives who giggled like schoolgirls and snatched up sequinned numbers for parties while their husbands were seduced by girls who wore jeans.

Francesca stood behind Clare for a while as she painted. The blonde girl had one arm wrapped protectively around her body so that her hand caressed her hip, while the other played nervously with a well-glossed lip.

'What do you think?' Clare asked, stepping back from the canvas so that Francesca could have a better view. She was blinking rapidly, obviously fighting back tears. 'It's not that bad is it?' Clare joked nervously.

Francesca shook her head vehemently, but it was too late. The flood-gates burst open and suddenly tears were streaming down her prettily made-up face, rivers of salt water stained blue and pink with mascara and powder. Her shoulders shook as she stood there, desperately trying to stem the flow with her little hands.

'What's wrong, what's wrong?' Clare took hold of Francesca's shoulders instinctively and used the towel that she had been wiping her paint-stained hands with to dab away at Francesca's face. She didn't push Clare away but wrapped her arms around her and buried her face in Clare's sweater as though she were an old friend and not, though Francesca had no reason to know it, a woman who had so recently laid her husband. Clare guided Francesca through into the sitting-room and cleared a space so that she could sit down. As Clare sat down next to her, Francesca clung to her again and Clare started to stroke Francesca's flower-scented hair as words finally began to tumble out with the tears.

A tear lingered on Francesca's cheek, a perfect half-sphere waiting to elongate and fall. As she burbled on, the tear still hovered there, unmoving. Clare was transfixed by the tiny orb, in which swirled rainbow patterns, and it was almost unconsciously that she leant forward to kiss it before it had time to run away.

Francesca drew away, still holding on to the tops of Clare's arms, and looked at her, eyes wide.

'I'm sorry,' Clare said, blushing.

'No, no, I am,' Francesca dabbed at her tears. 'I shouldn't be bursting into tears on you like this.' She leapt up from the sofa and paced the room, searching frantically through her handbag for a tissue that wasn't sodden with salt water and mascara. Her shoulders were still shuddering with the emotion.

'What exactly is wrong?' Clare asked again.

Francesca sank back down on to the sofa again and hesitated for just a moment before throwing herself back into Clare's arms.

'I just don't know what I do wrong,' she sobbed. 'I just don't know. He spends all his time away from me looking for new places to buy and do up and when he comes home he just locks himself in his study. He isn't interested in me any more. I just need someone to make me feel . . . well, feel anything again . . . I feel like I'm bloody dying for someone to touch me.'

Their eyes locked. Francesca was studying Clare intensely, as if her last exclamation had been not an observation but a challenge. A challenge to Clare.

Clare swallowed nervously as Francesca's gaze continued to pierce her eyes. The muscles at the back of Clare's neck twisted with the tension of this endless moment while each wondered what to do next.

Moving closer, Francesca brushed her lips across Clare's cheek and the sensation of this unexpected return of affection was not of the lightest of kisses but of a burning firebrand in the shape of her lips.

Francesca sat back to look at Clare once more and a moment of silence and stillness hung between them again before she finally drew Clare's lips to her own.

Clare had never kissed another woman before and had been genuinely embarrassed when the tear on Francesca's cheek had tempted her to touch the blonde girl in anything other than a friendly way. As Francesca placed a slender, well-manicured hand on Clare's knee, Clare's first instinct was to pull away. But for Francesca, Clare later thought, this was definitely not a first time. The surprise Clare had seen in her eyes was merely pleasure at the arrival of an unexpected opportunity. She passed a hand over Clare's hair as though she was calming an anxious pet dog.

'Don't think about it,' Francesca whispered. 'Just let it happen.'

Clare closed her eyes, shutting out the looming face. Francesca kissed Clare's jaw, her chin, her nose, her ears, her eyelids, her forehead and then her lips again. Finding Clare's lips still tightly shut, Francesca made a little noise of amusement before she set to work at prising them open with her tongue. Moments later Clare's own tongue poked tentatively out to touch the tip of Francesca's, and they wrestled them for a moment like the teenagers in boarding schools, experimenting with 'how to kiss'. It was different from any kiss Clare had experienced before. Francesca's touch was lighter and gentler than any man's touch . . . And she had no stubble!

Her tears had all but dried now and when she drew away from Clare again, to check her eyes for surprise, Francesca was laughing slightly to herself.

'What are you laughing about?' Clare asked her.

'Oh, I'm not laughing about anything,' Francesca replied. 'When I laugh it's just because I couldn't possibly smile any wider.'

She leant towards Clare and gently pushed her backwards so that she was lying on the sofa. Clare's body was so stiff with tension that Francesca was reminded of a wooden doll. As the kissing continued, Clare kept her eyes tightly shut, still wrestling with the fact that she was being seduced by a woman. But soon a warm hand was creeping beneath Clare's sweater, caressing a nipple through her bra. It hardened in spite of Clare's misgivings. Clare let Francesca's hands wander curiously over her body for a moment or two, unsure of what she should be doing in return. Exactly the same as Francesca was doing to her, Clare guessed, but the move from kissing to actually caressing another woman's body seemed just too great to make. Francesca was patient, nuzzling Clare's cheeks, whispering encouragement until she felt arms close around her back. She struggled out of her top at the earliest possible opportunity and laid her half-naked torso against Clare's. She had pushed away Clare's clothing so that their bodies rested in some places skin to skin.

'Touch me, Clare,' Francesca murmured. 'Touch

me.' Her words were softened by her quickening breath. Clare moved a tentative hand from Francesca's back. Francesca shifted to make herself perfectly accessible. She held herself slightly above Clare, to her side, jutting out her chest so that the target couldn't be more obvious.

Francesca's breasts were smaller than Clare's, encased in a peachy lace-edged bra that was almost invisible against her lightly sun-kissed skin. Clare began to caress them, in the way that Francesca had caressed her, but she was obviously taking too long about it because, before Clare could steel herself to tucking her hand inside the bra and actually touching Francesca's delicate nipples, the blonde girl had reached around and unhooked her bra herself.

'Kiss them,' Francesca begged her nervous lover. 'Suck them.' Tentatively, Clare lifted her head to the proffered breast and flicked out her tongue. Francesca's tiny pink nipples stiffened immediately at the mere suggestion of Clare's caress. She pulled Clare's head closer to her breast and thrust one of the quivering buds into Clare's mouth. 'Bite it,' she commanded. Part of Clare's mind still fought against the suggestion but she gently closed her teeth together on the stiff little bud. 'Harder,' Francesca rasped. 'Harder.'

As Clare paid attention to her breasts, Francesca's hands had crept lower. She was wrestling with the belt of Clare's jeans, deftly unfastening the button fly. Suddenly noticing the shift in focus, Clare tried to push the fiddling hands away.

'No, don't,' she pleaded. 'I really don't think I want . . .'

'This?' Francesca had already broken down her defences. The hair of Clare's pussy seemed to stir with excitement as Francesca's fingers brought her up in goosebumps of nervous desire.

Clare closed her eyes as Francesca's fingers tangled in her hair, waiting for the inevitable. Soft fingers on her clitoris made her bite her lip and sent arrows of tingling electricity all over her body. Francesca kissed Clare again, thrusting her tongue inside Clare's sweet mouth as her fingers echoed the action down below.

'Aaaaaah!' Clare broke away from her lover's mouth and threw back her head.

'Shhh,' Francesca whispered. 'You're so nice and warm inside. So wet. You're enjoying this. You really are.' A peculiar tingle ran down Clare's spine at these words. 'Just lie back and relax. I'm going to make you come . . .'

Automatically, Clare raised her hips so that Francesca could pull her jeans completely out of the way. She had been wearing no knickers under her painting trousers, as she often didn't. Francesca smiled her approval and now licked her lips as she contemplated the task ahead and ducked her head down between Clare's thighs.

With the first flick of her tongue Francesca found Clare's clitoris. She bucked her hips upwards with the surprise. While they were thus raised, Francesca grabbed her lover's buttocks and used them to lift the girl still further, so that she could more easily reach her target. Her tongue moved more slowly now, up and down the shiny shell-pink of Clare's vulva, tantalising her clit. Her eyes fixed on Clare's. Every cell in Clare's body was beginning to vibrate.

'Let go.' Francesca demanded. 'Let yourself come. I can feel you're almost there.'

She was wet from her nose to her chin. It wasn't all saliva. She returned to her frantic tonguing. Clare's hips bucked ever higher again, to drive Francesca's tongue into her. Clare grasped the blonde head, forcing it further between her shaking thighs. Francesca didn't have to ask Clare to come again. Suddenly, her body took over. Every muscle was tensing and relaxing, tensing and relaxing so quickly, it was as if she had been plugged into some ecstatic source of electricity. Clare's mind sat back to watch as she shuddered and covered Francesca's face with sticky sweet come.

The orgasm over. When Clare had finished shaking with its tremendous power, Francesca crawled up the sofa and kissed her gently on the lips. Slowly Clare licked them dry, tasting her own love juice mingled with Francesca's sweet tongue.

'Good?' Francesca asked.

Clare nodded in reply, her eyes still closed. Still breathing heavily.

'Really good?'

'I think so.'

'Right. Now it's your turn,' Francesca said. 'Let's go to bed.'

Clare had never seen another woman's vagina. Francesca reclined on the bed nonchalantly, her legs slightly parted, waiting for Clare to come between them. Her pubic hair was slightly darker than the hair on her head – as if Clare hadn't guessed that Francesca's fluffy blonde locks were dyed! – and the darker hairs were already slightly damp. Clare found herself strangely pleased to see that she hadn't been the only one to enjoy her first Sapphic orgasm!

'What are you waiting for?' Francesca asked, eyebrows raised.

A picture of Daniel lying on that same bed flashed briefly in Clare's mind. She could tell this woman to go now but Francesca slid forward so that her feet touched the floor and her sex was at the edge of the bed. She reached out her hand and twisted a little of Clare's long brown hair between her fingers. Francesca's face was glowing with desire. She communicated a message to Clare which she couldn't ignore now.

Clare knelt between Francesca's open knees and stared in wonder for a moment at the gently swelling clitoris and labia which were becoming more prominent through the hair even as she drew nearer.

'That's right,' Francesca breathed. She pulled gently on Clare's hair to bring her closer still.

Clare gazed at the picture before her. What should she touch her with first? Her fingers or her tongue? Like a baby, which puts every new discovery into its mouth, Clare chose her tongue.

She began by carefully taking some of Francesca's soft brown curls between her teeth, nibbling and pulling them gently, not so hard as to cause any pain. Francesca moaned contentedly and her hips rose slightly from the bed – Clare was doing OK. The musky female aroma that Clare had smelled on her own fingers after masturbating was rising gently towards her from Francesca's vagina, enticing Clare further down. Taking Francesca's slender hips in her shaking hands, Clare made the dive, stretching out her tongue to its full pink, hard length, licking and then penetrating. Tasting that familiar perfume and being delighted by it, Clare licked and licked, faster and faster in response to the excited moans which came from the girl on the bed. Her enthusiasm soared as Francesca writhed on the sheets, just as Clare had done on the sofa. Clare continued her actions, now more confidently and harder until Francesca's hands clutched her head and she cried out.

Up and down Francesca's hips bucked, so that Clare felt her tongue was fucking the girl. Then Francesca pushed Clare away from the centre of her pleasure and pulled her up on to the bed so that they were level and their mouths touched. Flipping Clare over on to her back with surprising strength, Francesca ground the mound of her pubis against Clare's, and they rocked back and forwards, Francesca's hands grasping for Clare's breasts, Clare's hands sweeping up and down Francesca's back, streaking them with lines that went first white and then pale red. Francesca was moaning, sighing, desperately clutching her lover's body to her own. Clare put just one finger into Francesca's vagina. The muscles there were opening and closing like a hungry mouth as Francesca soaked her hand. 'I'm coming, I'm coming,' she screamed. Clare pumped her finger in and out of the pulsing vagina and could hardly believe what she had done.

Afterwards when Francesca lay still on the shambles of a bed, her eyes closed in a contented doze, Clare wandered over to the dressing table and sat down. Her mouth and chin were smeared with Francesca's vibrant pink lipstick. Clare studied the figure on the bed for a moment. Francesca's arms were raised above her head. She was a smooth unbroken curve that ran from the tips of her fingers to the soles of her feet, gently undulating where a tiny waist became a swelling hip. Clare walked over to the bed and sat down beside her. Francesca's eyelids fluttered as the bed dipped slightly beneath Clare's weight. Clare let the back of her fingers follow the line she had made with her eyes.

The gentle touch awoke Francesca, smiling, from her sleep, and she wrapped her arms around the other girl's waist, pulling her down beside her on the bed. They looked at each other for a long time, noses almost touching as they lay face to face, gently caressing each other's hair, earlobes and cheeks. Clare marvelled at the fragility of the body that had just given her such strong pleasure. Outside it was just beginning to rain.

'Are you okay?' Francesca asked. Clare's expression was still that of someone who was not sure that she had done the right thing.

'I'm fine.'

'Can I stay?' Francesca continued. 'I mean, your boyfriend won't be coming back and if he does come back unexpectedly, you can always say that

I came round drunk and you were obliged to offer your benefactress a place to stay. He won't think . . .'

No, thought Clare, no one would think . . .

'But won't Steven be expecting you?'

'He thinks I've gone back to London,' Francesca hissed. 'And he's probably gone out to pick up some local tart anyway . . .'

Her words made Clare wince. If only she knew. But Clare had made up her mind about one thing now anyway. After that afternoon, she would never be able to see Steve again.

'Okay,' Clare told her companion, 'you can stay. But you'll have to go first thing tomorrow.'

Francesca nuzzled Clare's neck in appreciation and pulled her slender body closer. She was asleep within minutes, contently moulding her belly to her lover's back. Clare gazed open-eyed into the darkness of the night.

# Chapter Ten

*LIFE IS WHAT* happens when you've made other plans. The next day, when Francesca had finally gone back to London, Clare wandered down to the harbour, diligently avoiding the fatal café on her way. Since she couldn't find her foldaway stool in the chaos of the flat, Clare doubled up her jumper to make a seat on the cold, grey stone wall, and balanced the board she used for an easel on her knees. Graham wanted still more sea scenes. The woman in America was ordering them to be sent all over the place for Christmas. Clare mixed up a job lot of sea-green on the inside of her paint-box lid and began to work on three small scenes at once, like a factory production line. She hadn't got much further than three wishy-washy horizons when he appeared.

'Fancy meeting you here.'

'Yes, fancy.' Clare replied.

Steve was swaddled against the cold in a huge cream fisherman's jumper. He sat down beside her on the harbour wall without being invited and cast an eye over the paintings.

'Hmmm,' he said. 'Not bad.'

Clare didn't say anything. She continued to paint. A seagull appeared on all three paintings, then a fishing boat, so far out to sea it was just a streak. He must have thought her silence a little odd, but what could she say? – 'Hey, Steve, since we were last together I've learnt about your first and second wives and been to bed with your third wife – and do you know what the really funny thing is, she was easily as good as you . . .'?

It was Steve who broke the silence. 'Shall we go for a coffee?' Clare shook her head and continued to paint. She copied the colours of a nearby fishing boat.

But Steve remained beside her, smoking a Marlboro light and flicking the ash into the murky green water that swirled below them, until, finally, she just couldn't help asking: 'So, where have you been lately?'

Steve took a long drag on his cigarette. 'Here, there and everywhere. I've been very busy.' Of course he didn't say that he'd been hiding out of the way while his wife was in town. 'I saw you from the window of a house the estate agent was showing me around, just over there. I'd been hoping that we would bump into each other again. You didn't give me your number.'

'I don't have a phone,' Clare replied.

'You should get one. I've missed you.'

'I'll bet you have.'

But the anger that she felt towards him for having lied to her – well, for having been economical with the truth – was quickly ebbing away even as they sat there, getting numb bums on the wall. Clare knocked over the jar of water that she had been using to rinse her brushes and as they both reached to right it at the same time, their hands brushed together. The electricity was most definitely still there. Clare set down her easel by her side and turned towards him. He searched her face eagerly for the words which played on her lips.

'Shall we go and get that coffee?' she said finally.

He smiled broadly. It was a goal to him, Clare guessed.

Clare reached out to push the golden brown hair from his forehead. So, he was nearly forty, eh? He didn't look it. By the time she was sitting opposite him in the café, she was already undressing him with her eyes. Tracing a path with her tongue down to the snake tattoo on his hip. As if he sensed that the chill was abating, Steve took the hand that had smoothed his hair and gently bit Clare's forefinger as he stared straight into her eyes.

'You've got such pretty hands,' he told her. 'Dangerous nails.'

She thought about scoring passionate lines up his back and wondered if she had left any marks the last time they were together. She smiled.

'Tell me about yourself,' Clare said suddenly, daring him. 'I feel like I don't know anything about you . . . Who dubbed you Steve the Snake? When did you lose your virginity? How old are you? Have you ever been in love?'

'Questions, questions.' He significantly chose to ignore the last one. 'I'm twenty-one.'

Clare rolled her eyes. She wasn't going to get

anything out of him. And what good would it do anyway? If she asked him whether he was married, if she confronted him about Francesca, he'd hardly be inclined to take Clare back to his hotel room again. And that afternoon that was definitely what she wanted, no matter how much she told herself it was wrong.

'Do you want to . . .?'

Clare nodded before he could finish the sentence and they headed for the car.

'Your place or mine?'

'Yours,' Clare said, adding quickly, 'My place is a tip.'

To his credit, the boy on the reception at the hotel retained an exceptionally discreet demeanour as Steve rushed the dark-haired girl through the door. They began to kiss in the sumptuous gilded and mirrored lift and Clare couldn't help opening her eyes just slightly to enjoy the spectacle of their kiss from all angles. This time there were going to be no torturous tickling, featherlight touches. Clare's jeans were undone before Steve's key was in the lock.

'I really have missed you,' he murmured into her crotch, rubbing his chin against her pussy like a real cat eager to be fed. He hoisted Clare on to his shoulders and started to nibble at her clit, while his fingers began their excellent play. His stubble tickled against the inside of her thighs. But this wasn't going to last long. Steve was just too hot and had hardly begun to waken Clare's body when he started fumbling with the belt of his own jeans.

'Condom!' Clare reminded him with a giggle as he stretched himself full length along her body and began to push against her urgently. He cursed, rolled off Clare and rolled one on. He came back to the bed and threw himself backwards on to it.

'Right,' he said, 'your turn on top!'

Without hesitation, Clare straddled him and hovered above his dick but first playfully placed her own finger in her crotch. 'Ready?' she asked. Steve's cock twitched as if in reply, then stood to attention, like a glorious pole on which there really should have been a flag. Slowly, tantalisingly, Clare began to lower herself on to him.

At first, she took only the tip inside her, waited for a moment, then began to slowly ease herself up again. Steve shuddered at the sensation. The next time, Clare went a little deeper, her thighs quivering with the effort of resisting the urge to plunge him into her, right up to the hilt. Steve's hands began to creep up her legs. His eyes were closed in delirious pleasure.

By the time she made her third journey down, it had already become too much. Clare sighed in ecstasy as her bottom brushed Steve's balls and he pushed upwards at the same time, driving into her, impaling her, filling her with his gorgeous cock. Clare's body was racked with a delicious quaking, every nerve ending vibrating, singing with joy. She arched her body backwards and held the position, relishing the feeling before she carried on.

Steve's eyes were still closed. Beads of sweat were beginning to gather on his forehead as Clare rocked on his prick, her once measured breathing now coming in shorter and shorter gasps. Determined to heighten the sensation still further, she reached behind her and teased his sac with a careful stroke from her long fingernails. He moaned urgently. His shaft reacted by twitching inside her. Her pussy tightened in response.

'You feel just too good!' he told her, grasping hold of her waist with both hands to help her move up and down even faster. Clare grasped handfuls of her own hair as the pleasure began to reach a dangerous intensity. Her vagina grasped Steve's penis.

'Slow down, slow down! I'm going to come,' Steve groaned as his hips drove him further into her one more time. But it was too late to slow down now. Clare's pussy contracted again and again, and her orgasm burst from her like a peal of laughter, pumping the hot come out of him while her own love-juices trickled down the inside of her thighs.

'I have to spend more time with you,' Steve panted as Clare collapsed on to the bed beside him. 'This weekend. What are you doing this weekend? I'm not going to have to work . . . we could go Barcelona—'

'Barcelona?'

'Yes, come with me.'

Clare figured that she had probably had all the sexual adventures she deserved that week, but she told him that she'd love to. She wasn't really in the right state of mind to ask herself how.

'Why am I saying "yes"?' she asked herself out loud.

'Because I've put a spell on you,' he said.

Steve dropped Clare off on the corner again and she walked the rest of the way to the flat. Daniel's car was parked half on the pavement outside the flat. She hadn't expected him back so soon, but the last thing she'd thought to find, when she let herself into the flat, was that he was sitting drinking tea on the sofa with Francesca.

Clare froze at the door.

'Daniel let me in,' Francesca said cheerfully, nonchalantly, chirping as she had done on the day she first came to commission the painting. 'I hope you don't mind but we took the liberty of looking at the picture while we waited . . . I love it, it's really very good.'

Well, Clare thought, I haven't added anything to it since I saw you this morning but 'I'm glad you like it' was all she could manage out loud.

'I'll make you some tea, shall I?' Daniel asked as he headed for the kitchen, leaving Clare alone in the sitting-room with Francesca.

'Where've you been?' Francesca hissed. 'I've been here for hours . . .'

'What are you doing here?' Clare countered.

'Well, first of all I wanted to see you but also I left my credit cards at the hotel. When I got here I found you weren't in and then, when I went back to my car, the damn thing wouldn't start so I couldn't go up to the hotel – it's too steep to walk in these shoes . . .'

Thank God, Clare thought.

'Daniel's been trying to help me to fix the car but it's really totally knackered. I don't see why I should drive a Volkswagen when Steven swans around in that bloody TVR of his. I rang him at the hotel to see if he'd come and fetch me but he wasn't answering his phone. The lads at the site said he'd gone back there . . .'

'Probably with some tart,' Clare laughed ironically, remembering how Steve had taken the phone off the hook after the first twenty rings, before they spent another hour in each other's arms.

Daniel came back into the lounge with some tea. He was smiling soppily at Francesca. Besotted. A strange, jealous spike twisted in Clare's heart and she wondered if she should tell him that the vision of loveliness on the sofa wasn't a real blonde. Francesca was smiling soppily back at Daniel and carefully crossed her legs to give maximum exposure to her well toned thighs, while appearing to remain totally innocent to the effect this was having on the assembled company. It was strange how very different she was in public and in bed, Clare thought.

'Well I suppose I had better be getting back to the hotel,' Francesca sighed after a few minutes of strained conversation. 'Are you sure it won't be too much trouble for you to drive me, Daniel?'

'No, I'll drive you back,' Clare butted in. 'Daniel's been driving all day.'

Daniel opened his mouth to protest, at which Clare shot him a look that suggested she thought he was the one who would get up to something if he was left alone with this girl. He closed his

mouth. Francesca raised a flirtatious eyebrow at
Clare. As they left the flat, Francesca stood on
tip-toes to give Daniel a kiss on the cheek. When
she pulled away, a cerise circle marked the spot
where her lips had been. Daniel was enchanted,
charmed, grinning like an idiot from ear to ear.
Clare gave him a little kick in the shin as she
passed.

'Are you angry?' Francesca asked her when
they were safely in the car. 'I got about ten miles
down the road when I thought that I just had to
come back and see you again. I didn't think your
boyfriend was going to turn up so soon. I thought
we could spend the afternoon in bed and . . .'

'Francesca, I . . .' Clare didn't know what to say
but she had an awful feeling that her life was
about to get horribly complicated.

'My mind has been racing all day,' Francesca
continued, 'and I've had a fantastic idea.' She
paused for effect. 'I want you to come away with
me, this weekend. I've got to go to a knitwear
show in Paris to get some stuff for the shop. The
show's on Friday. We can fly out in the morning
and come back on Sunday.'

'I can't,' Clare said flatly.

'Why not?'

'I've got things to do . . .' Like spend a weekend
in bed in Barcelona with your husband, Clare
didn't add. It had suddenly become clear why
Steve was going to be unexpectedly free from
business meetings and rounds of golf. Barcelona
with the husband or Paris with the wife? It wasn't
the kind of choice Clare had to make every day.

'What things to do?' Francesca persisted. 'What

can you have to do that would be more fun than spending a weekend in Paris with me? Think of it, Clare. All that shopping!'

Clare rolled her eyes. 'I'm not sure I . . .' She chickened out of voicing her hesitation about their relationship and said instead, 'How would I explain it to Daniel?'

'Easy,' Francesca gushed. 'Just tell him that a girlfriend of yours has won a weekend away and that she's got no handsome beau to go with. I'll ring you up to make it sound kosher.' She'd thought of everything. 'Just imagine it, Clare. The Louvre, the Champs Elysees, Notre Dame . . . Galéries Lafayettes!'

'He won't believe that.'

'Of course he will. Steven would believe it.'

Yes, Clare thought, but he had his own motivations for wanting Francesca out of the way.

'*Pleease.*'

'I can't afford it,' Clare said at last.

'You don't need to afford it. I've already got the air tickets. It's you or my PA – and she's got a fear of flying and a hairy upper lip. Come with me. Please. Please. Please.'

'Okay. Okay.' What was Clare letting herself in for? What was she going to tell Daniel? What was she going to tell Steve?

'Right, we're flying from Gatwick. Here are the details.' She handed Clare a slip of paper. 'Can you meet me there?'

Clare nodded.

Francesca was clasping her hands together in joy. 'You won't regret it,' she said, 'This is going to be incredible. We are going to have so much fun.'

Suddenly Clare realised that she was automatically driving in the direction of the hotel she had left just an hour or so earlier, so she asked Francesca where they were supposed to be heading. On the way there they passed the building site Steve was working on. Clare prayed that he was still there and not back in his room at the hotel. Fate, fortunately, was on her side.

# Chapter Eleven

*STEVE WAS DISAPPOINTED* when Clare told him she couldn't make it to Barcelona after all. When she said that she was going to Paris, on a ticket won in a raffle, with a friend from school that she couldn't let down, he remarked, 'That's a real coincidence, my . . . friend is going there as well this weekend.' He told Clare that he could cancel the tickets anyway and that he could always use some golf practice. Daniel was far less happy.

Francesca, as promised, had telephoned the flat pretending to be an old girlfriend from school. Daniel was confused as to why Clare should want to spend a weekend away from him with a girl that she hadn't spoken to for four years. Clare assured him that they had actually kept in touch. But to Paris? he moaned. He asked why this schoolfriend couldn't drag up some willing man to see some of the most romantic sights in the world with. He begged Clare not to go. Promised to take her there himself one day and when she refused to give in he went into a sulk which lasted the whole week and hadn't let up by the time Clare got him to drive her to the station, where she was catching the train to Gatwick.

Clare made it to the airport with plenty of time to spare and sat in a café, drinking coffee and wondering if she was doing the right thing. What a crazy situation! Before meeting Steve, Clare thought she would never get involved with a married man, let alone a married woman. Not just a married woman, but a woman she hardly knew. If her mother could have seen her! If Daniel could have seen her, she thought a little sadly. Maybe a weekend away from him would actually help them both, give them a chance to miss each other, see what they had been taking for granted. On the other hand, it could be a complete disaster.

An hour after Clare arrived at the airport, just as she was entering another 'this could be a complete disaster' phase and about to give up the game and go home, Francesca materialised from the midst of a crowd of giggling children. She was carrying three cases, as opposed to Clare's one, rather scruffy bag.

She was effervescent, smiling benevolently at the kids as they got under her feet and in her way. She dropped her bags and kissed Clare on both cheeks.

'Bonjour, *ma chérie*,' she trilled.

'Bonjour,' said Clare.

'Have you already checked in?' she asked, eyeing Clare's conspicuous lack of luggage.

'No.'

'Oh. Well, come on then,' she said briskly. 'You can take one of these bags. I want to make sure we get a non-smoking seat. Travelling in the smoking section is just such a nightmare . . .'

Clare nodded but wondered if she would be able to get to Paris without needing a fag to calm her nerves. She had only flown a couple of times before.

'I'm so excited,' Francesca said, bouncing up and down. 'And the hotel I've booked is fantastic. You'll love it. I got a suite. Our rooms both connect on to a central area so you can go off and do your own thing if you want . . .'

'My own thing?'

'Yeah, French guys are just so sexy. They only have to open their mouths to say something in that accent and . . .' Francesca gave a little shimmy.

'I know just what you mean,' Clare laughed. She couldn't help feeling a little relieved. She had not been sure that she could have amused Francesca on her own all weekend long.

Francesca was right. The hotel was fantastic. As she gabbled incomprehensibly in French to the receptionist, Clare stood with their luggage and gazed around the entrance hall. On her last trip to France, a weekend in Boulogne with the sixth form French group, Clare had stayed in a cockroach-infested fleapit of a youth hostel. Now here she found herself in a five-star hotel near the Champs Elysees, in a road just off the Rue François Premier, one of the most amazing streets in Paris. As they had been driven from the airport in a taxi, Francesca had pressed her nose to the window, pointing out the boutiques as they passed. 'Nina Ricci,' she gasped, 'Chanel. Oh, my goodness, there's Inès de la Fressange's place. I read about that boutique in Vogue. We'll go there tomorrow. Sells very classic clothes apparently. She's bound to have something that's you . . .'

'Yeah, but not something to suit my bank manager.'

'Who cares? It'll suit Steven's bank manager. Emotionally he's a wet fish, but financially . . .' Francesca laughed and flexed a plastic card.

Clare had barely recovered from the marbled splendour of the lobby when she had to begin gazing in wonder again at the room Francesca had booked for the weekend. It was quite unlike all the Holiday Inn-style hostels Clare had stayed in before, where the decor was uniformly beige and the only extravagance was an extra carton of cream by the teasmade. This room was a riot of colour! And it wasn't just a room! The suite Francesca had promised had two bedrooms, a lounge and even a tiny kitchen with a freshly stocked minibar. In the communal area, a green leather suite dominated. Francesca kicked off her shoes straightaway and leapt on to it, testing its bounce. The walls were hung with limited edition prints. Clare lovingly fingered one of an abstract still life that she was sure she had seen and admired in a London gallery a couple of years earlier. Francesca didn't seem quite as fazed by the décor as Clare was, wrapping the scarf she had been wearing on the plane round the neck of a large, black marble panther that guarded the door. She was now reclining on the rich green leather sofa, pointing the remote control at the widest television screen Clare had ever seen, which brooded in the opposite corner.

'They've got a great porn channel here,' Francesca commented. 'Just in case we can't think of anything better to do . . .'

A bottle of chilled champagne was waiting in a silver bucket on a glass-topped table. Clare popped the bottle open and poured two glasses.

'Vive la France,' Francesca sighed happily, raising her glass to the view. 'I love these big windows, don't you?' She had leapt up from the sofa and was now drawing back the raw silk curtains and looking down on the street below. 'And Paris is the perfect place for big windows. Look at the view, Clare. That woman with the dog down below . . . I'm sure it's even wearing a Chanel collar – everyone here is just so chic!'

Clare joined her at the window and couldn't help recalling the woman with the dog who had walked past the window in St Ives . . . and her surprised husband.

'Kiss me,' Francesca commanded. They were still at the window but Francesca just didn't care. Clare dutifully took the pale face in her hands and caressed the waiting red mouth with her tongue. This was going to be one hell of a weekend.

They dressed for dinner. Clare didn't have anything which Francesca deemed suitable for her plans that evening and so she lent her lover a green dress. Clare had never worn green before but Francesca assured her that, with the natural red highlights in Clare's hair, which she insisted was worn up, it looked great. So great, Francesca told her, that she was torn between letting Clare out at all or keeping her to herself in bed. They had already shelved the idea of an afternoon at the knitwear fashion shows in favour of that. Francesca was wearing cream. A tightly-fitted suit, beneath which she wore nothing but a push-up bra that gave her a fairly respectable cleavage. Her hair was also piled up and pinned with pearl-studded grips, revealing the soft line of her long neck.

'Classy,' Clare whispered as Francesca emerged from the bedroom, still applying her lipstick.

'Should be,' she replied, 'it's Yves Saint Laurent.'

'Are you ready?' Clare asked, pulling on the gorgeous grey cashmere coat that Francesca had also lent her for the occasion.

'Almost,' came the reply as Francesca disappered into the bathroom again.

Clare slipped the coat back off and turned on the television.

At once she was hit by a barrage of high-speed French. She used the remote control to flick through the channels to find something she could summon up the interest to attempt to understand. The news looked depressing. On one channel there was a comedy programme that she had seen on television in England a year earlier. It was dubbed. Clare watched that for a few moments, amused more by the poor synchronisation between sound and vision than the programme

100

itself. That programme finished. Francesca was still in the bathroom. Clare continued to channel surf.

Suddenly the screen was full of moving parts which Clare couldn't quite relate to anything she'd ever seen before. It took a couple of seconds for her to realise that she had stumbled upon the porn channel Francesca had spoken about. On screen was a close-up of an impressively large penis penetrating a shaven vagina, accompanied by sounds of moaning that could have been in any language but were probably Swedish. Clare was so transfixed that she hardly noticed when Francesca finally emerged, looking no different from when she had last paraded for Clare's approval, and sat down beside her on the green leather couch. She slung an arm casually around Clare's neck and settled in to view. They wouldn't be going out for a while longer.

The scene cut to a hilarious routine with six thirty-something porn stars cavorting across a hockey pitch in gym-slips that just barely covered their frilly white knickers. The girls on the sofa collapsed into hysterical laughter, especially when Francesca suddenly burst out, 'That's exactly like my old school uniform!'

'Oh no,' the tears of laughter rolled down their faces as they thought about it.

'But if we'd flashed our knickers like that we would have been in detention for a week!'

'We had to wear those disgusting thick blue gym knickers over our normal pants whenever we were on the hockey pitch,' Clare told her companion.

'At lunch-time, I used to do handstands deliberately to show mine off whenever the boys from the school up the road walked past.' Francesca said.

'Was it an all girls' school?' Clare asked her.

'Yes, a convent actually,' she replied. 'And I boarded.'

'You? A convent girl? I can't believe that. What a nightmare!' Clare sympathised.

'What do you mean? I loved it. I've only got a brother, so the girls at school were like the sisters I always wanted to have . . .'

'Was that where . . .?'

'Was that where I first got off with a girl?' She completed Clare's question, her fingertips sliding gently down over the bare skin of Clare's neck to her collar-bone. A delicious shiver ran through Clare's body at her touch.

'Yes, it was. I had a crush on the geography teacher for years. She was fresh out of teacher-training college when I arrived in my first year and compared to all the crusty old nuns she was a goddess in her thick glasses and crêpe-soled shoes.'

Clare laughed.

'I think what attracted me to her was the fact that she seemed something of an adventuress. She'd spent a year in South America between university and teacher-training school, building fishing pontoons for the natives or something worthy like that. And she had nice hair. Dark with red bits . . . like yours in fact.' She ran careful fingers over Clare's neatly piled-up hair. 'But that whole affair came to nothing – except for a grade A in O'level geography.'

Clare groaned. 'I got a C. Our geography teacher was an old bag. But that's beside the point. Tell me. Tell me who it was and how it happened.'

'OK.' Francesca had returned to the business of gently stroking the other girl's neck. Clare relaxed back into the deep soft sofa and Francesca's arm. 'Well. In the sixth form we finally got to move out of the main boarding house which permanently smelled of sweaty feet and Dettol, and into a building on the other side of the playing fields. We had our own rooms and shared a study with one other girl. My best friend, who was as thick as the proverbial planks, had left school at the end of the fifth form to do the Season and all that crap. So, I was left without a study mate and wound up with a girl called Anna. She was a year older than me. Had spent most of her life in South Africa, so when she returned with her family she was a year behind at school. Just a year older, but somehow she really stood out from the rest of the girls in our class. She had a real air of sophistication. We were allowed to wear our own clothes in the sixth form and instead of slavishly following fashion, she was always so classically stylish. While the rest of us were just recovering from disastrous perms which were the craze in our fifth form, she had long straight white-blonde hair that hung down her back in a plait like a rope. By the time she arrived at school, I was completely into boys, having a "relationship" with a boy from the local grammar on Saturday afternoons when we were allowed into town in threes. I gave him a blow-job in the ladies' loos at the bus station.

103

'Boys were definitely becoming more interesting. I had grown out of the geography teacher thing and took great pleasure in pillorying the "real lesbians" with the rest of the girls. But Anna was just so beautiful, so serene. She made me blush when she spoke to me. I was getting that kind of reaction to men but to a girl again . . . that really freaked me out.'

Clare nodded, understanding the confusion Francesca must have felt only too well.

'Did you ever feel like that at school?' Francesca pulled back from Clare a little to study her reaction.

'Well, no actually. I was always very much into boys.'

'Complacently heterosexual until you met me, eh?' Francesca laughed. 'Oh, do you really want to hear about this? It's nearly eight. We should really be going out.'

'No, carry on. I'm intrigued!'

'OK. But don't blame me if you start to feel jealous.'

Clare gave her a playful punch on the arm.

'So, we were sharing a study, Anna and I, except that for me, studying was now becoming quite out of the question, because her being there totally robbed me of my ability to concentrate. The study was a sort of sitting-room as well, with two big armchairs that had springs poking out to jab you in the kidneys if you tried to get too comfortable. She would sit in the one by the window and I would sit in the one by the book shelves, watching her as she read. Always sitting perfectly, with her back straight while I sprawled with my legs across one of the chair arms. Sometimes I used to watch her for what seemed like ages, thinking that she didn't notice me, because the sun which came in through the window slightly obscured her face. But, of course, she had noticed me watching and one day she asked me why. She just came straight out and asked me if I fancied her. Of course I wanted to crawl under the threadbare rug and die when she said that. I denied it. Reminded her that I had a boyfriend – boy being the operative word, and told her that I wasn't staring, it was just that I was gazing into the distance while I tried to remember the conjugation of some French verb.

'By the time I had garbled all that, she was standing right in front of me. She put her book down on the table and sat on the arm of my chair. She reached up and unfastened her plait like the heroine of some film, letting her hair fall around her face. She stroked my cheek with her long-fingered hand and then pulled my face towards hers.'

Francesca fell silent.

'What happened then? Did she kiss you?'

'Yes.'

'And then?'

'I don't know. I can't really describe it, I . . .'

'Show me instead.'

Clare shifted position so that she and Francesca were eye-to-eye.

'Show me from the beginning.'

Without further prompting, Francesca cupped Clare's face in her hands as Anna had done hers years before and planted a very gentle kiss on the smiling lips. They pulled apart and studied each other for a moment. Then Francesca leaned towards her lover again and repeated the action, lingering there this time until Clare's mouth opened under the exquisite pressure of her fluttering tongue. Clare's hand tangled in Francesca's golden hair.

'Mmm,' Clare murmured. Francesca's mouth tasted of the freshness of toothpaste and was cool from the water she had been sipping as she spoke. Their tongues stroked each other languorously. 'Then what did she do?'

Francesca finished kissing Clare's mouth and began to let her lips wander over her cheeks instead. She moved up to Clare's eyes and kissed her carefully on her fluttering eyelids. Then down the side of her face. Kiss, kiss, kiss. Clare instinctively leaned her head to one side so that her neck was more exposed to Francesca's travelling lips, which were hotter now, much, much hotter. Clare's back prickled with pleasure as she felt Francesca's teeth close gently on her throat.

'Then what did she do?'

Clare could hardly speak now as Francesca bit carefully at the nape of her neck, where her hair began. Momentarily she felt almost paralysed. Streamers of prickling desire unfolded to either side of her spine.

'Oh, my . . . that feels incredible . . .' Clare murmured.

Francesca began to fumble with the zip at the back of Clare's dress, tugging it down until Clare's shoulders slipped free of their covering.

She pushed away the straps of Clare's cream silk slip so that her shoulders were completely bare, ready to be kissed. Francesca kissed along her lover's breastbone until she came to the centre. With just a little more persuasion, the dress slipped right down, taking Clare's underclothes with it, and her breasts rose up to greet Francesca's descending lips. Her nipples were erect; had been erect for some time.

'Then what did she do?' Clare's voice was barely a whisper as Francesca encircled first one nipple and then the other with her mouth. Her tongue flicked lightly across the reddened buds, while her hands cupped the full orbs of Clare's breasts and stroked them lovingly.

'More,' Clare insisted when Francesca began to move away. 'More. Don't stop.'

Francesca continued to tongue her lover's nipple, by turns biting it teasingly, but her hands had another purpose now. They were creeping up Clare's stockinged legs, under the fluid jersey hem of the dress. Francesca reached Clare's suspender belt and moved her hands beneath the lacy straps which held her stockings up. For a moment or two she savoured the pleasure of having Clare's beautiful, firm thighs beneath her hands, before moving higher still.

A small laugh escaped Francesca's lips when she realised that, once again, her companion was not wearing any knickers. She twisted her fingers in the silky hair, traced them down the warm, waiting labia, then up again, to Clare's aching clit. Lazily she circled the little bud with a finger, watching with great pleasure as Clare closed her eyes and bit her painted lip.

'Carry on,' Clare breathed. 'Please carry on.'
She let her legs fall more widely apart. Francesca
traced a languorous path between Clare's swollen
lips, making her lover sigh with pleasure.

'You're such a tease,' Clare growled.

Francesca's finger found the entrance to Clare's
desire and slipped slowly inside. The muscles of
Clare's pussy tightened happily around their
visitor.

'You're so wet,' Francesca breathed.

'Getting wetter.'

Francesca dragged her finger backwards and
almost withdrew, then she slid it back in again,
happily feeling Clare's muscles contract.

'Do it faster.'

Francesca obeyed the command and began to
work up some speed.

Clare tensed the muscles in her thighs. She
pressed her high-heeled shoes into the plush
cream carpet to steady herself as Francesca
increased the pressure and the pleasure.

'Faster.'

Francesca added another finger. The room was
silent except for the wet noises Clare's body made
as the fingers slipped in and out and the sound of
two girls breathing deeply. Francesca as aroused
as she was arousing.

Suddenly, Clare's hand flew down to her pussy
and she gripped Francesca tightly around the
wrist, helping her to plunge deeper, holding her
hand in place. Her breathing had lost its regular
pattern. Her lips were flushed deep red.

'Ohmigod!'

Clare head jerked backwards while her hips jerked up to meet Francesca's hand.

'I'm coming, I'm coming, I'm coming!' she shouted exultantly.

'I know!' Francesca laughed, feeling that Clare definitely wasn't faking. When she had finished, Clare slid from the sofa to the floor and they lay together on the cream carpet, bodies entwined.

'I'm going to have to do my hair again,' Francesca stated flatly after they had been lying still for a couple of minutes.

Clare burst into a fit of the giggles.

They ran together to the bathroom and stripped off their clothes to take another quick shower. As Francesca carefully soaped her hot and relaxed body, Clare asked, 'Did she really do all that to you?'

'Yes,' Francesca replied.

'And did you have an orgasm?'

'Not quite like that one, no.'

Clare was strangely pleased about that.

Francesca knew Paris well, but Clare didn't, and before they went to the restaurant Francesca had chosen for their first evening, Clare insisted that they take a quick dash around the sights in a taxi. Francesca moaned, but she gave in.

'But the Eiffel Tower?' Francesca made an exasperated face. 'It'll be swarming with tourists.'

'I am a tourist, remember,' Clare said, silencing her with a kiss.

Clare let Francesca do the talking. She had spent a few months in France after leaving school, at the insistence of her father.

'To finish me off,' Francesca laughed. 'The best way to learn a language is to have an affair with a native, though I don't think that is exactly what Daddy had in mind for me . . . *Ici, s'il vous plaît, monsieur.*' Francesca had the taxi stop in a street next to the river.

While Francesca fiddled with the francs, Clare clambered out of the taxi and stood transfixed by the beauty of the silently weaving Seine. The river was lined by lights whose reflections glittered and flickered like flames beneath the surface of the water. A large, flat, glass-roofed boat was passing by, bedecked with yet more shimmering lights. It was full of tables, diners, people dancing their way around the Ile de France. Clare tried to suppress a memory which was forcing its way into the forefront of her mind. Daniel's birthday. A cruise on a restaurant boat down the smelly old Thames. She'd worn a stripy jumper and talked with a stupid accent all evening to make up for it not quite being France. He had thought that was hilarious. His best birthday ever – especially the French knickers Clare showed him at the end of it.

'Come on, dreamer,' Francesca caught her arm. 'It's just a short walk from here to *la Tour Eiffel*!' Now it was Francesca's faux French accent that was making Clare laugh. 'We'll go to the top, just for you, I'll point out the red light districts and then we are going to go and have dinner! My stomach is rumbling!'

'Oh, you are such a romantic!' Clare said sarcastically.

As predicted, the Eiffel Tower was swarming

with tourists and there were long queues to go to the top. But Clare didn't mind. It was just so incredible to her that they were there at all. She tipped back her head and looked up through the ironwork to the sky. The struts were glistening with bulbs.

'It's so big,' Clare murmured.

'Who?' was Francesca's automatic reaction.

When their turn came to get into the lift which would take them up to the viewing platforms, Clare made sure that she was by the outer edge of the glass-sided elevator. She didn't want to miss anything, and somehow being able to see out would make her feel less claustrophobic, which was a very important consideration since the guides were packing people into the lift by the dozen. About halfway up she heard Francesca exchanging French words which didn't seem to be pleasantries with a guy who stood behind her.

'He pinched my bum,' she explained. 'I wouldn't usually complain but I didn't fancy him at all.' She manoeuvred herself away from his roving hands and wedged herself next to Clare at the window.

'Fantastic, isn't it?' Clare breathed. 'I can't believe I'm in Paris.'

'Believe it, beautiful,' Francesca whispered. Their eyes locked in a secret smile for a second before the lift doors opened and its contents tumbled out into the cool night air.

It was so cold. Francesca and Clare clung to each other for a little warmth. The wind whipped their hair around.

The viewing platform was closed in by wire

netting which slightly obscured the view, but all the way around it was a desk which bore information about the landmarks you could see out there in the dark. Paris lay beneath them with all its best bits illuminated. The Sacré Coeur was clearly visible, its white majesty lit up by floodlights. Notre Dame was also lit, and though Francesca seemed fairly uninterested in the view, Clare made her promise that the very next day they would visit that famous cathedral. 'And light a candle for our salvation,' Francesca added with a smile.

'And the Louvre, we've got to see the Louvre,' Clare insisted. Francesca nodded. 'And the Musée d'Orsay; some of my favourite impressionist paintings are there, and the Pompidou Centre – that has some great modern stuff – Matisse and co.'

Francesca was covering a mock yawn. 'You can see all that provided I get to go to the Chanel boutique tomorrow and I get my dinner right now!' As if in agreement, her stomach chose that moment to give a impressively loud rumble.

'Point taken,' Clare replied, feeling pretty hungry herself by now. They took the lift back down and flagged a taxi to take them to the restaurant, which was on the other side of town.

The restaurant that Francesca had chosen was an old favourite of hers. It was dark, intimate. The arched ceiling was covered in red velvet! As they entered the maître d' nodded his regards to Francesca as though she were a regular.

'I came here on my honeymoon,' Francesca

explained, and Clare was surprised to feel a thrill of excitement and not hurt.

A young waiter pulled out Clare's chair, a move which always took her unawares and usually resulted in her nearly ending up on the floor. Francesca smiled at the lack of grace and the astonished look on Clare's face when the waiter also shook open her napkin and placed it on her lap.

The leather-bound menu looked bewildering. Clare racked her brains for the schoolgirl French that would save her from ending up with a plate of veal or horse meat. She recognised *les cuisses de grenouille* – frogs' legs – and panicked. They were about the only item on the menu she would be able to pronounce!

'Have snails,' Francesca commanded. 'I think they've got aphrodisiac qualities.'

'No way!' Clare said firmly. 'And they're not aphrodisiacs anyway. You're thinking of oysters.'

'Have you ever tried snails?'

Clare shook her head.

'Exactly. And to think I thought you were the kind of girl who would try anything once . . . Maybe I should have brought my PA along after all,' she teased.

'OK, OK. I'll try one,' Clare gave in. They couldn't really be any worse than mussels, she figured.

Francesca ordered for both of them and folded the menu. She handed it back to the waiter who had taken their order with a slow wink. Clare kicked her beneath the table with a pointed toe.

'Pack it in, will you?'

'You're not jealous, are you?' Francesca purred.

The waiter returned with a pair of instruments which looked not dissimilar to eyelash curlers. As he turned to go again, Francesca picked up the shell-holders and chased after his retreating bum with them. Clare clasped her head in her hands in mock embarrassment.

'He was asking for it. Wearing those tight trousers . . .'

The snails arrived, steaming and garlicky, and Clare wrinkled her nose in distaste. She had already changed her mind. Evidently as well versed in molluscs as she was in everything else, Francesca deftly scooped one out of its shell with the dainty fork and held it to her companion's firmly closed lips. She popped it into her own mouth instead and swallowed it with an exaggerated look of divine ecstasy on her face. 'They're delicious,' she purred. 'Like chewing a clitoris.' They fell about laughing. Clare ate three after that.

The rest of the meal was a little more palatable. Francesca had ordered steak, rare and dripping with blood. Clare had gone for fish and left half of it, much to the disgust of their waiter who asked her several times if anything was wrong. Clare could hardly tell him that the thought of the night ahead with Francesca had made her too nervous to eat, though half the time she wasn't sure that the theatrically languorous way in which Francesca took each mouthful was entirely for her benefit anyway.

As they sipped their coffee, Clare's, of course, *au lait*, she noticed that Francesca no longer seemed interested by her at all. Her doe eyes were now narrowed like a cat's. She was scanning the faces in the room and not tremendously subtly at that. The restaurant was full of couples, though Francesca and Clare were the only pair of girls.

'All couples,' Francesca confirmed disappointedly. 'But what do you think of those?'

A pair of young waiters leaned louchely against the bar, moaning no doubt that the customers were taking a long time to leave that night. They looked very similar – perhaps brothers – and were good-looking in that Gallic way. Thick dark hair, darker eyes. Big nosed.

'And you know what they say about men with big noses,' Francesca winked. 'I'll call one of them over to get the bill and we'll ask if *le service est compris.*'

'Francesca! No!' Clare protested feebly. 'They're waiters! And anyway, I don't fancy either of them.'

'You can put paper bags over their heads. I'll have the taller one first and if you really don't like yours, we'll swap over at half time.'

Clare really wasn't sure, but it was too late. Francesca had clicked her fingers and the tall one was already on his way.

Clare focused her slightly drunken eyes on his strong hairy forearm as he leant on the table to listen to what the beautiful blonde had to say.

After a brief exchange in French, which lost Clare as soon as Francesca had said *Bonsoir*, the waiter wandered off again and Francesca rose from her chair in readiness to leave. 'They have to stay behind to tidy up,' she explained. 'But he's

115

given me directions to a really great club and says that they'll meet us there when they've finished. We'll go back to the hotel and change first, if you like.'

'Francesca, I really don't know ... I'm tired. Can't we do this tomorrow night?' Clare was terrified by the thought of being left to make stilted conversation in a variety of pigeon languages with the shorter waiter while Francesca had her way with the other one. What was she getting them into now? Francesca blithely ignored her companion's apprehension.

'I've got a black dress that would look really great on you ...' she chattered on regardless as she guided Clare out of the restaurant and into the night.

# Chapter Twelve

BACK AT THE hotel, Clare headed straight for the mini-bar to calm her frazzled nerves. Francesca and Clare had waited for two hours at the club before the waiters finally showed up but now Jean and Bertrand were comfortably ensconced on the green leather sofa, with Francesca between them. She had her leg crossed towards Bertrand, her shoeless foot twitching predatorily, brushing from time to time against his trousered calf. Clare opened another bottle of champagne and filled four glasses. She sat down opposite the other three but wasn't on her own for long.

'See you later,' called Francesca as Bertrand swept her up off her feet and carried her giggling into the darkness of her room. Jean had made his way over to Clare and was now perching on the edge of her chair. His arm snaked around her shoulder and he fixed her with his chocolate-brown gaze. She told him that she didn't normally do this kind of thing but to no avail, since his English seemed to be as bad as her French.

'Let's just kiss.' He had that phrase nailed. He bent down towards Clare and passed his tongue over her lips. Despite herself, she found her mouth opening to let him inside. He tasted wonderful, and Clare had to admit that the way he smelled was starting to turn her on. He used the same aftershave as a guy with whom she had had a passionate affair the summer before going to art school. That guy had taught Clare pretty much everything she knew – except of course, that large chunk of carnal knowledge to which she had been introduced by Francesca.

Unconsciously, Clare began to let her hands wander over this new body, starting by running her fingers through his thick brown hair. Jean, however, was working to a faster timetable. His hand was already at the zip down her back, tugging it open. Clare wondered whether she should protest, but the thought was lost in the persuasion of his kiss. Soon, her own fingers found the buttons of his shirt. She pushed it out of the way and continued to explore.

She couldn't disguise her pleasure at the sight of his bare chest.

Jean was firm, brown, with the well-defined muscles along his torso from his ribs to his belly that show a man who really takes care of himself. His chest was covered with a layer of curling hair against which she just couldn't resist rubbing her face. A line of the hair continued down along his stomach, disappering into his trousers, which were beginning to tighten around the flies with the strain of his contained excitement. She drunkenly followed the line down with hands, teasingly keeping away from his belt buckle.

'Let's go next door,' Jean murmured into her neck as he pulled her to her unsteady feet. They staggered into Clare's bedroom, not letting go of each other. He picked up a bottle of champagne as they passed the fridge, maintaining contact with her silk-stockinged legs as he knelt down to open its door.

'Now we are ready . . .'

Clare didn't need to drink anymore, but fortunately, Jean had thought of plenty of other uses for the bubbly stuff. The green dress had long since been discarded. Clare lay on her back, still wearing her stockings. Jean carefully eased off the knickers Clare had put on to go to the restaurant. Just a little gentle persuasion and she languidly opened her legs. Jean knelt between them, still wearing his trousers, fiddling with the foil around the top of the bottle as lovingly as if it were a foreskin.

Pop!

The cork flew out of the bottle and ricocheted against a chandelier, sending it into a tinkling crystal symphony that continued long after the cork had fallen back to the floor. Just like a mutual orgasm, Clare thought. Hers, of course, being the chandelier, not quite so explosive but much more prolonged.

Now Jean had his thumb over the top of the bottle and he was shaking it backwards and forwards, sending jets of foam whirling up into the air to land on her body which tingled with cold and delight. Clare shrieked and writhed under the fountain of fizz, thrashing her head from side to side, catching droplets in her mouth.

A smile spread slowly across Jean's face. Quickly, he parted her legs again and directed the jet straight at her sex. Clare gasped for air. The surprise of the sensation made her want to snap her thighs together and open them wider still, all at once. But the shock was short-lived. The power of the pressure inside the bottle quickly subsided and Jean had to resort to pouring the champagne over her, dribbling the last of it between her labia.

He licked his smiling lips, a prelude to what she hoped he was about to do next.

'*J'ai soif*,' he whispered, leaning forward to take a drink.

Like a cat drinking milk he lapped at her. His tongue was so strong, Clare didn't last two seconds before she felt the urge to squirm. But more was to come. He sucked at her clit, taking it right into his mouth as no one had ever done before. Clare felt as if it had suddenly sent out a network of nerve tentacles that covered her entire lower body, tracks of ecstasy that reached down the inside of her legs to be raced along by the bolts of electricity that came each time Jean's tongue hit the button. Clare was crawling backwards up the bed, twisting up handfuls of the sheets as she went in the delicious agony of passion. As she tried to slip away from him, Jean grasped her waist in his powerful hands to pull her back down towards his tongue.

'Oh, no, oh no, oh no!' Clare panted. She couldn't possibly wait any longer. But then Jean's tongue was replaced by two fingers. He licked them first, for extra lubrication.

Jean's fingers began rhythmically sliding in and out of her soaking vagina, slowly at first, then faster and faster. Clare thrashed from side to side, moving her hips down to meet his fingers at each thrust. Her breath escaped in short gasps, punctuated by cries for mercy which she didn't want. Opening her eyes briefly, she saw, and heard, that Jean too was panting. His face was flushed, his pupils wide with pleasure, as he continued to work in and out of her, pausing only to massage her engorged clitoris with his thumb.

'Oh no, oh no.' Clare sat up suddenly. She clamped her hand like a vice around Jean's wrist and held his fingers within her as the first waves began to come. Stars danced inside her eyelids. The sound of the blood rushing around her head filled her ears.

'Aaaaah,' her grip tightened as an orgasm exploded within her body, flooding her limbs with pins and needles. Blood raced from one extreme to another until finally her grip on Jean's aching hand relaxed and her body slumped backwards on to the bed.

Such incredible pleasure from one hand. Afterwards, collapsed in exhaustion on the bed, Clare asked him, 'Do you play guitar?' He looked at her blankly. She smiled contentedly. He hadn't even managed to get his trousers off – what a gent!

It was obvious from the noise floating into the centre of the suite that Francesca and Bertrand were far from finished. Clare had wandered out of her room to the mini-bar and couldn't help noticing that Francesca hadn't bothered to shut her door. This was yet another first for Clare after her first Sapphic situation and her first real 'French kiss'. She had only ever seen two other people having sex in porn films and you don't really get to see that much in those. But suddenly she found herself, gin and tonic in hand, standing at the door of Francesca's room, watching her having it off.

Francesca and Bertrand were both totally naked. For a moment Clare just relished the contrast between Francesca's pinky white skin and his which was doughnut brown. Bertrand was lying on his back, his feet towards the door. Francesca sat on his chest with her back to the audience, blocking Clare from Bertrand's view. His erection was incredible. Claire had never see anything quite as big . . . Her mind flicked back to a memory of Francesca's sex. It would be interesting to see how this one went inside.

Francesca raised herself up from her sitting position and shuffled backwards on her knees so that the tip of his penis hovered at the entrance of her pussy like a sacrificial dagger. She reached down and took it in both her hands, guiding Bertrand towards his target which she then opened wider with carefully manicured fingers.

'Oh my . . . aaaaah.'

She had lowered herself down on the first thick inch. The rest of his shaft was still plainly visible between them, as if it were a bar holding them apart.

Francesca lowered herself a little further,

burying another pulsating inch. Then another, and another. Each time she let out a little cry, half pleasure, half pain. Still unnoticed, Clare quietly took another sip of her ice-cold gin.

Suddenly, Clare felt a hand on her shoulder. A hand closed her mouth to stifle any noise of surprise. Now Jean was standing beside her. She had obviously been too long in returning to bed with his drink.

'*Pas mal*,' he muttered when he saw what Clare was watching. He wrapped his warm arms around Clare's waist and rested his stubbly chin on her shoulder, settling in to join her at the watch.

Bertrand had grown tired of that position and now had Francesca on her hands and knees, her bottom waving in the air towards the door. The familiar pussy almost seemed to wink. Now Bertrand's penis stood out straight in front of him. He parted her lips with his fingers and once again took aim.

This time there was no warm up. Bertrand plunged in, straight up to the hilt so that his scrotum swung forward to bump against her. Francesca let out a cry of delicious agony but threw herself back at him all the same as if even his eight inches were not enough. Bertrand increased the tempo of his thrusts. Francesca's head was thrown back, her mouth emitting a throaty groan each time he drove inside. His hands held her hips steady and pulled her back and back and back.

'Keep going, keep going.' Clare could see that Francesca had taken one hand off the bed to fondle her clitoris so that she lurched forward precariously now as Bertrand neared his resolution. Clare recognised the groan which said that Francesca was about to find hers.

Meanwhile, Jean had decided to create his own scene. Clare had hardly heard the unzipping of his trousers over the sound of Francesca's cries, but she soon felt the insistent nudging of his penis at her own overexcited labia. She was at just the right height, since Jean had taken his shoes off and Clare was still wearing a pair of Francesca's lethally high heels. She turned her backside up just a little and made herself steady by taking hold of the door-frame. Though she couldn't see his dick, Clare guessed that like Bertie's, it was bigger than average, because, even after the incredible climax she had just had, his initial entry stretched her just a little more. Clare exhaled in pleasure and reached behind her to hold him tight. After a few luxuriously slow introductory thrusts, Jean all too quickly speeded up to match his best friend stroke for stroke.

Francesca's animal moans were blending into one long squeal. Bertrand was fucking her furiously. In their frenzy they had lost all rhythm and crashed together, heads thrown back, mouths open.

'Hold me, hold me,' Francesca screamed. Bertrand flopped forward over her body, enveloping her in his arms as their hips jerked in ecstasy.

Jean and Clare came just seconds after the other pair. Clare would never forget Francesca's face when she turned around to see where Clare's cries came from. It was such a picture of shock, for just a second, before she burst out laughing and yelled at her spectators, 'You bloody peeping toms!'

Bertrand was still impressively hard when he withdrew his shaft, slick with the mingling of his semen and her come, from Francesca's body. Clare made a mental note to make sure that, later on, she got some of that.

The boys stayed the night at the hotel. Francesca was obviously paying so much money that the manager made no complaint when she rang up to order two extra breakfasts in bed.

'What do you want, Clare?' she called across the room. Clare shrugged her shoulders and let Francesca order. Francesca laughed, 'Oh, I forgot that you'll eat anything that comes!'

The next day, Jean and Bertrand didn't have to work at the restaurant until the evening shift, and while Bertrand and Francesca were happy to stagnate in bed all day, Jean agreed that Clare should see more of Paris, since it was her first time in the city, and he offered to act as her guide.

Strangely, in the daylight, Jean looked far more attractive to Clare than he had done across that crowded restaurant. His brown eyes were so friendly, perpetually crinkled up in a smile.

As they walked, he held her hand naturally and they talked falteringly. First trying to tackle each other's languages, which, on Clare's part at least was an unmitigated disaster, then both speaking English. He really wasn't that bad at all. He told her he was a student, studying business at a college in Paris, working nights at the restaurant to pay his way. When Clare told him what she did, he looked at her askance. She guessed that in Francesca's Armani casuals, she didn't exactly look the struggling artist.

'I, too,' he said awkwardly, 'I love to paint. I like to show you.' Clare smiled. It was a bit late in their acquaintanceship for him to be inviting her up to look at his etchings, but she agreed to go with him to his flat in the eighteenth arondissement after they had looked around the Louvre. Clare had thought that she needed a little more time to recover from the previous night's exertions, though Jean's hand, gently massaging the back of her neck as they looked at the Venus de Milo, quickly persuaded her otherwise.

They charged around the gallery, paying lip service to the exhibits Clare had always promised herself she would see. In a darkened room full of Egyptian antiquities, Jean's lips brushed lightly against her cheek. His hands grasped her waist as he pulled her across the room to look at a smooth marble cat. Beginning to burn, she sought his lips with hers but he moved out of range, teasingly. It was getting too much. Clare told herself that the Mona Lisa would be there another day and soon they were hurrying back into the cold afternoon and heading for the nearest Métro.

From the outside, the block where Jean had his flat was old, dark and damp-looking. There were about seven storeys, and Jean told Clare that his room was at the very top. She stood in the tiled entrance hall, looked up at the never-ending flight of stairs and shook her head.

'I don't suppose that's working, is it?' Clare looked at the impossibly old lift, but thankfully, Jean was already smiling and leading her inside. It was the kind of lift that she had only ever seen in movies. It didn't have the dull stainless steel doors of lifts in the tower blocks back home, but a wrought-iron trellis that closed with a rattle. You could see the stairs twisting around the lift shaft as they rose to the roof in the little iron cage, and Clare imagined a distraught lover, running round and round down them as the object of her desires took the lift to the ground floor and out of her life. The wonderful smells of evening meals cooking and freshly washed laundry drifted across their upward path from the rooms to either side, and occasionally they heard music, or animated conversation that she couldn't understand. To Clare, the whole thing seemed quite incredibly exotic.

At the seventh floor, the lift door strained itself back and Jean and Clare spilled out on to the landing. The door to Jean's room was varnished a rich coffee brown and on it was pinned a piece of yellowing card with the word 'Artaud' written on it in the peculiarly squirly handwriting of the French. Jean's name, in his handwriting, Clare discovered as he struggled with the key in the lock. It was a very stiff lock, but eventually it gave and the door swung open drunkenly on its ancient hinges. Clare stood in the door frame and gasped in surprise.

A shaft of yellow-red light cut right across the

bare wooden floor like a direct path to the centre of the sun. On their journey up in the lift, Clare had grown accustomed to the darkness and assumed that Jean's room would be equally shady, but here on the seventh floor they were a storey above most of the surrounding buildings and Jean's beautiful large window looked directly west. Clare ran to the window and strained her eyes against the evening glow to pick out landmarks. The whole of Paris was spread before her again, only this time it seemed that it was just for Clare and not for a thousand other tourists jostling her at a rail at the Eiffel tower.

The sight was all too commonplace to Jean. He was busying himself putting things away, tidying up while Clare took in the magnificent view. What a fantastic place this would be to paint in, she thought to herself. There was at lesat as much inspiration in the colour of this sunset over the city as she had found in the everchanging sea at St Ives. Clare breathed it in, trying to burn on her memory forever the picture of the sky turning pink over Paris in the autumn, before the sun disappeared for the night behind the skyline.

Jean had put on some music. Edith Piaf, her tragically romantic voice the perfect soundtrack for the moment. Without turning round, Clare heard him opening a bottle of wine, pouring out two glasses, walking across the creaking floor towards her. He put his hand on Clare's shoulder and planted a careful kiss on her smiling lips as he passed her a glass. They each took a sip, Clare grimaced at the bitter taste, he didn't, and they chinked their glasses together to toast the dying day. Goosebumps of excitement prickled all over Clare's body as his hand brushed her pony-tailed hair out of the way so that he could kiss her neck.

With the sun finally gone, Clare could now take a proper look at the room. Jean, who had tired of the view first, was sitting on the bed – a sturdy mahogany affair. As a matter of fact, the bed was just about the only thing to sit on. There seemed to be a chair by the door, but it was covered in clothes which had been flung off in a hurry in the race from college to restaurant shift. Above the bed, on a wall yellowed by years of tobacco smoke which must have started before Jean was born, hung a poster for an exhibition. The tiled mantelpiece was covered in postcards and photos. He pointed out his parents in their garden in Normandy, his younger sister. His pet dog.

There was no sign of any painting he had been doing. But then he knelt down and began to fumble under the bed for something. When he finally emerged, he had a sketchbook and a number of large pieces of paper in his hand. He flopped them on to the counterpane and motioned to Clare to look through them.

Clare fell on to the paintings like a vulture on to a cow in the desert. She adored looking at other people's paintings. Three years at college had taught her that you can see so much of a person in the way they paint. When you draw someone else you can't help but draw how you feel about them. Bold strokes for confidence, light strokes for sensitivity. Likewise, a self-portrait is simply the soul laid bare. Hungrily, she sorted through the scraps and sketches that poured from his book. Landscapes, animals, studies of the bricks and ironwork in the very building where he lived.

'Wow,' she enthused as she searched for the right word. 'These are really, really good! *Bon*. I mean *bien*. Oh, you know what I mean.'

Jean, meanwhile, had been under the bed again and now emerged with something new to show her.

'What do you think?' he asked, pushing the piece of canvas into her hands. She looked at it first upside down and then from its side to mock him. But this really was something. A nude, pictured lying on the bed from beneath which the painting had come, Clare assumed. A girl, lying on her side, propped up on one elbow. One arm stretched up and over her head. Her hair falling over the lower shoulder. Eyes closed. The face serene. Clare was surprised to feel what might have been a pang of jealousy. The casual composition, the care with which he had blended the colours, told her that this was someone special to him.

'What do you think?' he asked again.

'Who is it?' Clare asked.

'Oh, no one special.' His narrow, up-down smile said otherwise.

'A girlfriend?'

'She was.'

Clare looked at him. Trying to tell him that he could elaborate if he wanted to. 'But sometimes things don't work out . . .' he continued. 'You have to let them go . . . Have your life.' He took the painting from her hands again and slid it back beneath the bed. 'Meet new people.'

130

Clare nodded, slightly hazy from the wine. She suppressed the picture of Daniel which came into her mind. It occurred to her that it was actually the first time she had thought of him that day.

'I would like very much to paint you,' Jean told her.

'Me?' Clare was surprised. No one had ever asked to paint her before, even in three years at art school, not even Daniel. 'Me?' she said again.

'*Oui*.'

'When? I've got to go back to England tomorrow.'

'I start now.' He brought his sketchbook out from beneath the bed.

'Oh no. I can think of better things to do now,' Clare took the edges of his collar flirtatiously.

'No. I want to draw you first,' he insisted.

'OK. How do you want me?' Clare laughed.

'Nude,' he said seriously. She giggled at his pronunciation. 'Take your clothes off in there.' He gestured towards the tiny bathroom. Clare was surprised, but obeyed. When she emerged, he had set up an easel and was sitting behind it, sharpening pencils. She stepped in front of him, where he had arranged a couple of blankets on the floor, and then sat down. He glanced up and put her into the right position with a few hand gestures. She was sitting with her legs tucked beneath her. Leaning on one hand. She wasn't sure that she would be able to stay like that for long . . . or that she wanted to. As she heard Jean's pencil begin to scratch away at an outline, his dark brown head bobbing in front of her.

His eyes travelled the contours of her body and

yet she felt as though he wasn't properly looking at her. She pulled faux-sexy facial expressions to catch his attention, which met only with commands to sit still. It was strange and yet so very erotic. He was appreciating her merely as a form.

'I'm starting to get a bit stiff,' Clare said plaintively after she had held her position for a quarter of an hour. 'You're obviously not,' she added sarcastically when Jean failed to acknowledge her complaint. His eyes were now resting on her breasts. Her nipples had stiffened in the cool draught that edged in at the window and came under the door, but she was glad to be a little cold because she liked the way her breasts looked then, taut and firm. It was how she would like them to be immortalised. Her fantasy was to have them cast in bronze, but nobody had ever asked her if they could and she felt it would seem a little vain to suggest it herself. But, she thought, glancing down to see where Jean's eyes had lingered, they were definitely among her best features.

'Nearly finished,' he said, his concentrated expression breaking into a fleeting smile. 'And then I will have to mix some paint.'

'Are you going to use natural colours?' Clare asked him, remembering the painting he had shown her earlier.

'I'm going to paint you how I see you,' he replied.

'Blue with cold?'

The sarcasm was lost on him. Jean's hand was moving frantically again as he shaded something in with a very dark pencil. He sat back from the easel and studied his work. He smiled. It looked right to him.

'Can I see?' Clare asked.

'Not yet.' He had begun to mix watercolours in the lid of his paint-box. He was going to wash colour over the pencil outline. Clare ached. She longed to move, but every time she shifted even a little, Jean would complain that she was disturbing the shadows that he wanted to paint.

She needed to think about something to take her mind off the pins and needles. No, what she really needed was somebody to rub his hands all over her body until she felt as though the blood was moving around it again. Jean had lowered the easel slightly, so that now she could see most of his face. His lashes were so long. They swept across his cheeks as his eyes moved. Clare remembered first making contact with those eyes, in the restaurant, after Francesca had made arrangements for their foursome with Bertrand. Jean had been smiling, or, as she thought at the time, laughing at Francesca's audacity and Clare's markedly contrasting timidity.

Clare's gaze wandered across his head, revelling in the light bouncing off his hair. She looked at his ears – even his ears were cute. He had an earring in one, a tiny yin-yang symbol. She remembered almost having swallowed it the night before. His jaw was stubbly again. He had the kind of dark beard that needs to be shaved twice a day for a squeaky clean look, but she was glad he didn't look like that. The stubble emphasised the shape of his face, the cleft down the centre of his chin. It accentuated the smoothness of his lips. His tongue flicked out across the bottom one in concentration.

Clare closed her eyes and remembered the first touch of those lips on hers, forgetting now the apprehension which had accompanied that kiss. She remembered the taste of his mouth. Coffee, chocolate and champagne. His tongue cool from just having taken a swig from the bottle. The scent of his skin. The cologne he wore which was so familiar to her. The smell of his clean hair. The softness of it as she scrunched it up between her fingers while they were kissing and later, while they were fucking. A friendly feeling was gathering at the top of her thighs as she thought about the man now absorbed in his painting.

Jean smiled when he saw the faraway look on Clare's face. Her mouth had opened slightly. Her lips were a deeper red than they had been a few moments before and glistened with moisture. He liked them even better now. Her cheeks too were noticeably pinker. At this rate he was going to have to mix all his paints up again. He absently ran a dry brush across his own lips as he studied her. It felt good. Suddenly the girl before him was transforming from the subject of his study into the object of his desires again. There was no point in trying to carry on with the painting. He had been distracted.

Silently, Jean rose from his stool and crept across to where Clare was sitting, her eyes still closed. He got within inches of her, but she didn't seem to notice. Jean held out the brush he had in his hand and traced along the line of her mouth.

The edges twitched up in a smile as she realised what was happening. Her favourite fantasy was about to come true, only this time, she wasn't the one in control.

As if he could read her mind, Jean swept the soft brush from her mouth, down across her chin and on to her neck. From her neck to her collar-bone. The slight tickling sensation there made her hunch up her shoulders. By the time the brush had reached the level of Clare's breasts, Jean's mouth had taken up the same path.

His tongue tasted of the red wine they had been drinking and the cigarette he had smoked as they walked to his flat from the Louvre. It was a decadent taste, Clare would think later on, the taste of someone who appreciated all kinds of hedonism. His kiss was hard, crushing her lips, bruising them. Their teeth banged together slightly, making them break contact for a moment with a laugh. Her head tilted backwards under the force of his embrace. This was how she liked to be kissed. Feeling that the other person was stealing something from her each time his tongue entered her mouth. He had dropped the brush, and now abandoned her lips to let his kiss roam all over her face, as if he would never be able to touch her again and wanted to remember the way she was with all his senses.

'Oh . . . you . . .' Clare began to speak but gave up, letting herself melt into his arms which embraced the whole of her, his hands covering her body so well that she felt as if he had more than two. His hands swept up and down her back, then grasped at her breasts, fumbling for her nipples, even hurting them slightly. He was still fully dressed. Clare began the task of undressing him, struggling with the metal buttons that fastened his shirt and refused to pop out of the thick cotton without a fight. Growing impatient, he helped her, sliding his belt out from its loops, unzipping the black jeans that hugged his hips.

The jeans were unfastened. Clare pushed them down over his buttocks, taking the cotton boxer shorts with them. She moved her hands around and around on his backside, grasping the muscles that clenched as he wrestled her on to the floor so that she was lying beneath him.

'Jean, Jean,' she managed to pant. His trousers and boxer shorts were around his knees. His dick, now free, waved from side to side in a stately motion as he raised himself up to position Clare on the rough blankets. She opened her legs so that her inner thighs were either side of his strong, sinewy hips. The anticipation and excitement swelling within her seemed to be filling her chest, making it harder for her to breathe. Jean lowered himself back down, crushing her sensitive breasts. Clare delighted in the touch of the wiry hair on his legs against her own delicate skin. Jean positioned himself to enter her. Clare shifted too, to hurry on the moment. She lifted her hips so that her pelvis was touching his. Jean's hand snaked down between them, helping his dick to find its aim.

'Oh . . .' Jean's first eager thrust made Clare suck her breath in sharply. She tightened her thighs against his body and held him still for a moment while she relaxed and let him further inside. But he couldn't hold off for long and soon he thrust into her again. His face hovered above hers. She looked up at the eyes, now tightly shut. He was biting his lower lip as he pushed himself into her again, feeling the divine resistance of her vaginal walls.

'Ah,' he thrust again.

Clare clasped his buttocks. Clenched her fingers into his hard, firm flesh. He responded with a deeper thrust, a longer moan. She raised her body again and again to meet him. But still it didn't feel deep enough.

Jean stopped his frantic pounding for a moment and pulled her legs so that they were wrapped around his middle. He curled his knees beneath him and rocked backwards so that he was sitting up with her astride him. Clare released her legs and used her own knees to help her move up and down on his glorious cock.

'Aaaah . . . aaah,' he moaned as she rode him. His hands raced up and down her body. Clare twisted her fingers in his hair, the soft hair she had been dreaming of.

'Stop, stop,' he held her down against him, preventing her from rising up again. 'I'm going to come.' It was too soon, too soon, but Clare couldn't just patiently wait for the moment to pass.

'I don't care,' she cried, continuing to ride him. He rolled on to his back, so that she looked down upon his ecstatic face. She was totally, totally in control. She rode him faster and faster, ignoring his pleas for mercy, for her to slow down so that

137

they could come together. She wanted him to be in her control, wanted him to be unable to contain the feelings she provoked in him.

'Come, come,' she incited breathlessly, her words making it harder and harder for him to resist.

His hips were beginning to buck upwards. His moaning began to take on the familiar tone that told her when the crisis was drawing near. His eyes screwed tightly shut, in ecstasy, in pain, desperately trying to hang on until she came too.

'No, no,' he begged her, simultaneously grabbing her hips and pulling her down on to his prick, impaling her with his frantically jerking member. Driving himself as far into her as he could possibly go. Clare threw back her head triumphantly as Jean writhed in pleasure beneath her. His come flooded her body and ran down her legs. She fell forward on top of him, laughing ecstatically. He was one hundred per cent hers.

'I wish you were here for a longer time,' Jean whispered into Clare's ear as he wrapped his body around her narrow frame. The heat of his breath and the sincerity of his words sent a wave of warmth through her body. She didn't say anything in reply but put out a hand to gently squeeze his thigh. He kissed her softly on the edge of her jaw and settled down to go to sleep.

Clare slept so well in Jean's tiny flat that by the time she did wake up, she had almost missed the flight she was due to take home. They raced to the hotel to pick up Clare's things and found

Francesca lounging on the green sofa in her dressing gown, with Bertrand sitting on the floor beside her, his head on her lap. She was languidly eating chocolates, popping them into her mouth one after another. Her eyes were fixed to the television screen. While Clare raced about, grabbing discarded knickers and stockings, Francesca didn't seem at all bothered, since she had already decided that they weren't quite ready to go home.

'I can't be bothered with a race to the airport now,' Francesca sighed. 'Call Daniel and tell him that the flights your friend won were a bit dodgy and that there was no room on the flight originally booked. It's simple.' She was running her fingers through Bertrand's hair as she berated Clare. 'I've already told Steven that I'm going to stay in town to see another show . . . He didn't sound too bothered. Probably with some girl. The bastard.'

Francesca thrust the phone into Clare's hand and stared at her until she began to dial. Daniel wasn't in but for once he had remembered to put the answermachine on before going out. Clare waited for the tone and garbled a guilty message.

'Daniel, it's me. Flight's cocked up. Looks like I'm going to have to stay here until . . .' She glanced over at Francesca, who mouthed 'Thursday'. Ignoring her, Clare said, 'Tomorrow . . . Sorry about this, darling. Hope everything's OK. Miss you.' Clare blew a couple of kisses to finish the message.

'You're a better liar than my dear husband,' Francesca laughed. 'Now all we have to do is think up mystery illnesses to keep these two off work for another day.' She ruffled Bertrand's glossy thick hair as though he were a King Charles spaniel. Jean had settled into the sofa beside her and was grinning from ear to ear.

'Oh, well, let's hit *le vin*,' Clare sighed. Another day in Paris wasn't so difficult to resign herself to.

Jean and Bertrand rang the restaurant and claimed to be suffering from food poisoning. Picked up from another, less reputable establishment of course. Excuses made, Bertrand dragged Francesca straight back to bed, and she squealed in mock dismay until his hands and tongue reduced her to delighted giggles.

Clare stood at the floor-length window, looking down on to the street below. She wondered how Daniel would take the message. Hoped that he wouldn't be on his own when he played it.

Jean was sitting on the arm of the sofa now, dragging lazily on one of Bertrand's cigarettes. He reached out a hand to her and she took it. 'Who were you telephoning?' he asked.

In reply, she told him, 'Just the person I share a flat with. A friend.'

They spent the rest of the morning looking at the paintings they had missed out on the day before and the afternoon trawling around the Père Lachaise cemetery in search of Jim Morrison's grave. The tombs stood in rows like tiny terraced houses and Jean tried everything he could to entice her inside one of the dank ghost homes.

At eight o'clock, Jean turned to Clare and asked

140

her whether they should be getting back to the hotel to join the others for dinner. No, she told him, she wanted to be with him alone for a little longer yet. He smiled broadly and dragged her off to a Mexican restaurant where he had once worked. They were guests of honour, seated at the best table. The manager's wife fussed around Jean as though he were her own prodigal son. He was very well liked by everyone, in fact, Clare observed, as he knocked back yet another tequila on the house.

Finally walking back Jean threw an arm around her shoulders and Clare hooked her thumb through one of his belt loops. His hips undulated deliciously as he moved and she couldn't stop herself from sliding her hand across his beautiful ass. Clare thought about dancing with him in the club that first evening. His easy grace, so unusual in a man. She moulded her hand around one squarely perfect buttock. When he seemed to be taking little notice of her attentions, she gave him a tiny, hard pinch.

'You are making it 'arder for me to walk,' he laughed, stopping suddenly in the shadow of a tall building and slapping her hand way. 'Look at this.' He took Clare's hand and placed it firmly over his awakening prick.

'Don't you mean *feel* this?' Clare corrected, rubbing the hardening bulge at the front of his trousers. 'If I'm going to look, there has to be something to see.' She took hold of his zip and mischievously tugged it down. She slipped a hand inside and started to set him free.

'Oh, Clare, *non, non, non,*' he moaned in

half-hearted protest.

They were walking by the river, at a point where it was well lined by tall trees. It being late autumn, the leaves were almost all gone, but the branches still provided quite a screen. The street lamps weren't strong. Immediately, Clare could see a thousand opportunities for an al fresco fuck. But just then a gendarme meandered past. Clare hadn't seen him coming, since she was used to looking out for a completely differently shaped hat. Fortunately, Jean had spotted the impending disaster and swiftly steered her from the bench she had been leading him to.

'Wait until we are back at the hotel,' he told her.

Clare pouted out a petulant lip. 'I won't feel like it then.' The gendarme had walked on by, whistling. Clare began to tug down the zip of Jean's hastily closed trousers again.

'Clare,' he moaned exasperatedly.

'What about down there?' she asked. A few feet ahead of them, the path split in two with one branch going down towards the very edge of the river while the other sloped upwards towards a bridge. The riverside path was overshadowed by the wall which edged the other path. It was dark, unlit, screened from the passing river traffic by trees.

'Okay,' Jean consented.

They wandered off the well-lit path, Clare unable to crush the nervous feeling of dark places which had been with her for as long as she could remember, but finding that the fear only made her want Jean more.

She continued to struggle with Jean's flies as

they walked so that by the time they found the perfect spot his dick was already waving in the air, poised for action. Jean was fully behind the project now that they were out of the glare of streetlights and he crushed Clare against his body, grinding her lips beneath his as his hands roamed up and down. It was as if he was trying to imprint her curves on his memory for all time.

Clare couldn't wait. She was beginning to lift her skirt for him.

'Turn around.'

She did as she was told. Jean grasped Clare by the hips to steady her as she bent forward. He murmured with approval at the sight of her stockings, held precariously in place by an exquisitely lacy belt. She was wearing high-heeled shoes, but these were sinking into the mud and she still had to raise herself up on to her tiptoes to be in exactly the right position. His dick was now nudging at the entrance to her sex, already very wet and welcoming. Clare exhaled in delight as Jean plunged himself into her, right up to the hilt. This first thrust was quickly followed by another which pevented her from drawing a breath. She tottered forwards with the force. Jean took preventative action by turning her and himself so that when the next thrust came, she could brace herself with her hands on the cold stone wall.

'Aaaah,' Clare couldn't stop herself from moaning, though she knew the other path was so close that people passing would be bound to hear. She jammed her right hand into her mouth, biting her fingers hard to stifle the noise. But she soon found that she needed both arms to stop herself hitting against the wall. Jean had found his rhythm now and she could tell that he too was making one hell of an effort to keep it quiet. Accompanying each thrust, he squeezed her bare hips, using them as handles to pull her body closer to him. It felt so good to be making love outdoors like this, with evening strollers meandering by on one side and glass topped boats full of people out to see some interesting sights sailing by on the other. It felt so good, and so bad . . .

A boat's horn sounded close behind them. Clare froze momentarily but Jean carried on. They couldn't really see, could they, Clare wondered. No, the screen of trees was too thick and besides, if they could see anything at all it would be Jean's square bare buttocks, not hers.

But keeping quiet was becoming increasingly difficult. Jean was now clasping her tightly to him. Holding her body upright against him. Panting in her ear and biting into her neck by turns. Her arms flailed out in front of her in a desperate attempt to maintain some balance. Meanwhile, her lower body was letting itself go. Her vagina was burning. The muscular walls clenching, squeezing, grasping. Jean's faltering rhythm told her that he too was about to lose all semblance of control.

'Hang on, hang on,' she begged him. He slowed down as far as he possibly could but he had already passed the point of holding off. With the next thrust he pulled her upper body back against him tighter than ever, letting out as he did so an indescribably animal noise. Clare's breath was forced out of her body. She had the sensation of her heart slipping out through her mouth. Her lungs were empty, she gasped for air. Blackness started to creep in at the corners of her eyes.

'Jean,' she clung desperately to the wall as if she was about to fall off the earth. Jean powered into her. Three more long, desperate strokes before his sperm was ripped out from his balls with the power of his ejaculation, pumped out of his body by the eager muscles which surrounded his dick like an avidly sucking mouth.

Clare's fingers scraped down the stone.

They slumped against the wall, still joined together, breathing raggedly. Clare turned her face to meet his. They stood cheek by cheek. He tightened his hold on her, then buried his nose in her loosened hair and breathed her in.

Clap, clap, clap.

Clare looked up to see the source of the slow applause. Yes, they had been screened from the river, but not from the bridge and there stood the gendarme, with two of his friends. Jean straightened himself up quickly and they ran, laughing and stumbling, down the blackening path. They had run too far by the time Clare realised she had left her borrowed stilettos behind in the mud.

Francesca and Bertrand lay entwined on the green leather sofa again. Their naked bodies were lit only by the light of the television which flickered and danced along their complementary curves. When she heard the door open, Francesca looked up but didn't bother to cover herself at Clare and Jean's entrance, as Clare probably would have done in her position. Bertrand also looked up lazily from his resting place between Francesca's silky thighs. He looked knackered and Francesca looked frustrated.

Cursory greetings over, Bertrand was content to settle back down again but Francesca had already wriggled out from beneath him and was tripping across the room. She headed straight for the little kitchenette where Clare and Jean had gone to fix some drinks. Francesca slid to a standstill across the tiled floor and Jean couldn't help but find his eyes drawn to her breasts which still jiggled from her little jog.

'Nice evening?' she asked brightly, insinuating her naked self between Jean and the sink.

'Great,' Clare replied. 'And you?'

'Sort of.' She pulled a face which belied her words. 'A little bit boring actually . . .'

'Really?'

'Yeah.'

Francesca had snaked her naked arm around Clare's fully clothed waist and moulded her body against Clare's side while she cracked ice for their glasses. A splinter of the solid cold water flew off the ice-cube mould and landed on Francesca's bare breasts. She shivered exaggeratedly. Her breasts began to jiggle again. She caught Jean's attention once more and gave him a predatory wink.

Clare had a feeling she knew what was coming next.

Now Francesca slipped her other arm around

Jean's strong shoulders and pulled him towards her under a pretence of keeping warm. Picking up the game, he wrapped her in the folds of his fleecy jacket. Clare pulled a pouty face and offered Jean his glass.

'You're not going to bed are you?' Francesca asked when Jean let her out into the cold again while he took his drink. 'It's still early.'

'Bertie's tired,' Clare said meaningfully.

'Exactly,' replied Francesca. 'But he might perk up if something interesting were to start happening . . .' She tucked herself back inside Jean's coat. Something pleasurably hard twitched against her buttocks through his trousers. 'Isn't that right, Jean.' His eyes pleaded agreement. 'It's not nice to be selfish, Clare,' Francesca added as a final blow.

'I see, so now you've worn out poor old Bertrand you . . . OK.' Clare shrugged her shoulders and wandered out of the kitchenette, leaving Jean in Francesca's more than capable hands. The girlie giggles started almost immediately. Clare ruthlessly quashed the wave of jealousy that began to rise in her chest.

She took her place on the sofa beside Bertrand. He lifted his head like a somnambulent tortoise and let her slide her legs underneath. His eyes were glued to the television. Clare had definitely got the raw end of this deal. She let her gaze travel the length of his body. He was thicker-set than Jean. His thighs were huge, a rugby player's, covered in dark hair. His magnificent dick was sleepily curled between them. Clare let her hand trail nonchalantly across his well-muscled chest, while she sipped her drink and tried to understand the adverts.

'Mmm,' he murmured. His hand rose to hold hers straight away and he looked up with a smile into her eyes. Maybe Francesca was right. Maybe he was just waiting for something interesting to happen. He rolled over so that he was on his front, his amazing taut buttocks to the ceiling. He buried his face in her cotton-covered crotch and breathed her in as she stroked up and down his back. His hot breath between her legs was already beginning to make her clitoris hunger for attention.

Bertrand's arm lolled over the side of the sofa and his hand rested on the floor. Then slowly it began to creep up her leg. Carefully massaging a foot, then an ankle. Things were beginning to come to life.

A shrill peal of laughter erupted from the kitchen. Francesca was having a good time and Clare was determined not to be left out.

Tired of Bertrand's slow hands Clare manhandled him into a more useful position as best she could. He was very heavy but at last he seemed to get the idea. He lurched forward and fastened his lips on to hers. His kiss was far sloppier than Jean's and when he started to move down her neck. Clare surreptitiously wiped off her face.

Bertrand nuzzled the buttons of Clare's shirt, making strange, feral sounds as he did so. He was moaning something in French which she hoped was complimentary, while he relieved her of her clothes. Not quite Jean's gentle touch, but arousing in its own way, Clare thought.

'Jean, aaaahh!' came a disconcerting shriek. Clare's eyes narrowed. Francesca wasn't just pinching her man, she was putting her off the business now in hand. With this in mind, and since Clare was bigger than Francesca and so took up more room on the sofa, she decided that it was time to drag Bertrand off to the bedroom, like a tigress dragging an antelope home for the cubs.

He swayed unsteadily when he got to his feet. A bad sign. But no, his dick was actually reassuringly alert. Clare remembered seeing him in action the day before. Her sex suddenly became the control centre of her body.

'Come on, big boy.' She pulled him along by her bra which she had hooked around his neck like a lead. His large hands waved in front of him, grasping for her. She tantalisingly kept her body just out of his reach.

Inside the room, Clare whirled Bertrand around and he fell in an ungainly heap on the bed. As she closed the bedroom door, she encountered Jean and Francesca, en route to doing the same thing. Her eyes locked with Jean's momentarily. He gave an apologetic shrug. She stuck out her tongue.

Back on the bed, Bertrand had arranged himself into a sort of star shape. His dick was now poking straight up in the air like a television transmitter. Clare's pussy was picking up the signals. She sashayed towards him, flexing the bra noose menacingly between her hands.

'Come 'ere,' he said gruffly.

Clare climbed on to the bed and knelt with one leg on either side of this thick trunk. She lowered herself backwards so that his prick just touched the twin cheeks of her buttocks. His eyes rolled a little with tiredness and tequila. She wasn't having that, so she used the bra to cover his eyes. Each cup making a lens. He laughed at her ingenuity.

'Now you won't be able to see where I'm touching you,' she said in a low hiss. She straightened out her legs and, using her arms to steady herself, hovered over Bertrand's body so that no part of her actually touched him. She was going to make sure that there would be no comparison between her and her blonde-haired friend.

'Lie still,' she ordered. He didn't. His English wasn't great.

She arranged herself so that her long fine hair now reached down to brush lightly across his gormlessly smiling face. She scuttled backwards like a crab, dragging her locks along him. His hands stirred the air around her. She dodged out of their way. When he had given up his game of blind man's buff, she returned to her task, covering his body with the minutest of caresses like a warm southern breeze. His prick was still giving her a standing ovation.

Tired of that trick, she lowered her body a little further so that now she was gliding across him with her silken breasts. Her nipples, swollen hard, scored the path. When she crossed his face, his tongue flicked out to meet them and missed both. She laughed softly as she dangled her left breast carefully just a centimetre above his mouth. If he could sense its presence he wasn't showing it. Finally she just grazed the pink button against his bottom lip. His mouth opened to let her in again but she had already taken the prize away.

Hair. Breasts. What else did she have to touch him with but her hands? That was boring. It didn't take her long to come up with one final instrument of slow torture. Her legs shuddered as she brought herself into place for this one.

'What am I touching you with now?'

Clare brought her pulsing pussy in line with his curving mouth. Her pubic hair touched him first, causing him to wrinkle his nose as if he were about to sneeze. He recognized the musky smell of her womanhood instantly and this time, instead of reaching out to touch her back with his tongue as he had done when she offered her breasts, he refused. If she was going to torture him it was about time she had a taste of her own medicine.

Clare squatted further so that her clitoris almost rubbed his nose. She felt so wet, wet enough to drip on him if he didn't do something about it and quick.

He laughed a secret laugh. His tongue poked out just a tiny, tiny fraction of a centimetre between his sharp white teeth.

'Go on, go on,' Clare thought to herself.

The poised tongue flicked out, lightning fast to take in her clit.

'Yes.' Clare was very, very pleased.

Bertrand gave up his pretence of helplessness and grabbed her by the hips to help her stay still while he began to lick along the length of her

151

inner labia with smooth, deliberate strokes. She began to writhe, but couldn't move out of his way – his hands held her like a vice.

'Oh, yes, oh, yes,' she moaned, louder and louder, not exactly abandoned to the moment, but hoping Francesca could hear. 'Oh yes, yes, yes.' Her chant rose like praise to the heavens. 'Yes, yes, keep going. I'm going to come, yes, yes.'

From the next room came a similar song, but louder, louder and faster still.

'Yes, yes.' Clare began to bounce up and down a little. Bertrand was having trouble finding the spot. 'I'm going to come. I'm going to come.'

'Yeeesss!' screamed Francesca. 'Yeeesss!'

Suddenly Bertrand pushed Clare's pussy away from his face and shoved her backwards down his body so that her vagina was now directly above his cock. He brought her down on it with such force that she let forth a yell louder than anything she had ever yelled before in her life. Even when she had dropped a brick on her toe, aged three.

He began to move her body furiously up and down with his hands until she picked up the rhythm. Every thrust was accompanied by a note of increasing ecstasy now. The sounds from next door were blurring from her mind. Her focus now was between her legs. Bertrand was raising his body to each down-stroke from hers.

But still this wasn't enough for him. Clare found herself instantly on her back. Her legs first trying to keep her body moving to meet his, then giving up and flailing manically in the air as he powered into her, his huge cock filling her, stretching her.

She began to come long before he did. The

nerves in her body flattening and scrunching. Even her eyes feeling rather than seeing. Bright, brilliant colours played across her eyelids. Her blood thundered in her ears. So loud, so loud. Her blood, his breathing, her breathing, his semen.

Bertrand collapsed on top of her, exhaling a sigh like his last breath.

'Now,' he said, 'I am really tired.'

'Have a good time?' Clare asked Francesca when they met by the fridge.

'Yes, thank you. And you?'

'Oh, wonderful.'

They sipped their cold gin and tonics in silence for a moment. Each regarding the other jealously beneath their tousled hair. Funny how the two random guys they had picked up on the first night had suddenly become so exclusive to each.

Francesca laughed first. Spitting out a stream of gin and tonic with the loud 'ha' that exploded from her body. Clare swallowed hers before she took up the giggle and they fell into each other's sweaty arms.

'Quits?' Francesca asked.

'Quits . . .' said Clare. 'Especially now that I know I'm better than you are . . .'

'What?' The war was back on. 'Qualify that remark.'

'Well, if we had a machine like a clapometer that measured the volume of participants' reactions . . .'

'It was Bertie who was doing the work . . . You came first.'

'I bet I could make you come first.' Clare threw

153

down the gauntlet.

'Choose your weapon.'

'Tongues.'

'We'll need referees.'

Bertrand and Jean were dragged into the lounge and seated side by side on the green leather. Bertrand was struggling to keep his eyes open. Jean flicked idly through the TV channels still on air.

Clare and Francesca knelt opposite each other on the carpet, laying down the ground rules before laying down themselves.

'And orgasms not to be unreasonably withheld,' Clare added finally. 'No thinking of father-in-laws or husbands.'

Francesca agreed.

'Let's get into postion then.'

The girls lay down like a yin-yang symbol, nose to tail. Each nonchalantly raised one leg so that the other could get a tongue in. Jean flicked the television off and did the honours by shouting go.

Each girl began licking frantically at the pussy of the other, Francesca concentrating on the smooth labia, Clare going straight for the clit. As she felt her clit stiffen, Francesca was unable to stifle a moan. The moan was an incentive to drive Clare on but she too was already finding it difficult to concentrate on her task. She was still tingling slightly from the fuck she had just had with Bertrand. She should have waited until she had calmed down totally and not given Francesca the head start.

'Amsterdam, Berlin, Cairo,' Clare tried to think of a capital city for every letter of the alphabet.

'Durban ... no that's not a capital. Aaaah!' Francesca had made some progress. She was playing a similar alphabet game in her mind with the names of famous fashion designers and had got as far as Ozbek. But her tongue was tiring and she cheated, backing her mouthwork up with the surreptitious laying on of hands.

'You're cheating,' Clare hissed, pulling her face away from Francesca's sticky-sweet crotch for a moment.

'All's fair,' Francesca replied, using her tongue like a dick now. Straining with the effort of keeping it straight and hard but very pleased with the obvious results. Clare's head lolled back on the carpet. She clamped her upper thigh down on the side of Francesca's head in a desperate bid to halt the progress of a fast approaching orgasm.

'Give up. I give up,' she wailed. Moaning and laughing all at the same time. But Francesca hadn't finished with her yet. Her tongue vibrated wildly over the stiff little clit which she now almost sucked into her mouth. Clare's body twisted and turned from side to side. Francesca used her hands to keep her target steady. The buttocks beneath her fingers clenched tightly together and a new stream of pleasure was soaking Francesca's mouth.

Clare had lost the bet.

Francesca jumped up from the floor laughing at her vanquished victim who still rolled on the carpet, moaning and groaning as if she had been shot rather than just brought to orgasm. On the sofa, Bertrand had fallen asleep. Jean smiled wryly.

'Last one to bed gets Bertrand,' Francesca said.

All too soon it was Monday morning. As Clare rolled over to gaze in lazy wonder at the brown back of Jean against the clean white sheets she was suddenly hit with a hammer-blow of guilt. She had almost completely forgotten about Daniel. She hadn't even bothered to try and phone him since Sunday to make sure that he had received her message about her late return. He would probably be apoplectic with rage by now! What was Clare doing? She was throwing away everything she had with Daniel on a crazy bored wife and a French guy who really held no appeal for her other than the same aftershave as her first love and eyelashes long enough to shame a cow! Jean murmured and rolled over in his sleep so that he was now facing her. His mouth was curved in a smile. Clare remembered the evening in his tiny attic flat. She was going to miss that smile.

While Jean continued to snore lightly, Clare picked up the telephone beside the bed and dialled home. Two rings and then the answermachine cut in. Same message as usual. 'Daniel and Clare aren't here right now . . .' At least he hadn't erased her name from the tape.

Jean moved closer to Clare in his sleep and threw his arm around her waist. He was still smiling.

'Hi, Daniel,' Clare said to the answermachine. 'Just to say I really will be back later. Not sure exactly when but definitely today. Depends on availability of flights. Leave the chain off the door. Love you.'

Clare put the phone down and settled into Jean's sleepy embrace. The warm scent of his chest enveloped her. She told herself that she might as well enjoy it while it lasted. Daniel had probably spent the weekend boozing and playing football anyway . . . And absence made the heart grow fonder. Didn't it?

But Clare's heart touched down with the plane. She glanced across at Francesca, who looked similarly crestfallen. Francesca took Clare's hand and squeezed it.

'Stay in London tonight,' she pleaded. 'I don't want this to end.'

'I can't,' Clare reproached her gently. 'I'm already two days late! It's not fair on Daniel.' Clare stroked Francesca's face with the soft furry paw of the teddy bear she had bought for Daniel in the duty free shop as a peace offering. 'I'll call you tomorrow. And we'll see each other again soon, I promise.'

'How soon?' Francesca begged her.

'Soon, soon,' was all Clare could say as she steeled herself to go.

Clare had been thinking about her position on the flight home. She had to finish this madness. Francesca was obviously becoming too attached and it could only be a matter of time before she found out above Steve. Besides, there was Daniel to think about. Clare had decided that she wanted to be with him after all and so she had to play by the rules. That meant no more messing about. Within the next couple of days she would make sure that Daniel sat down with her and they talked seriously about where they had been going wrong. They would sort out the problems that their rivalry in work was causing. They could even move back to London if that was what it would take to make him feel happy with himself, and with her, again.

But Clare had also been thinking about Jean. On the coach journey home she took out again and again the scrap of paper on which he had scribbled his name and address and a tiny caricature of himself. Clare wondered if she would ever see him again.

By the time Clare arrived at the gates of the block where she lived, it was approaching midnight. She looked up at the windows of the flat and was curious to find herself relieved to see that none of the lights was on. Daniel was out, or he was already in bed. Either way, he couldn't have been too bothered about her late return.

Clare opened the door quietly, in case he was asleep, and didn't put on a light, for fear of awakening him. She tiptoed into the bedroom and threw herself down on to her side of the bed. He wasn't there. Must be out, she thought. She couldn't be bothered to get up again to turn on the light, so she undressed in the darkness, under the covers because it was cold, and was asleep within seconds.

# Chapter Thirteen

*SHE MUST HAVE* been very tired, because she didn't wake up until midday. The weak winter sun was streaming through the window, but it was freezing and her breath made smoky patterns in the air. And Daniel still wasn't beside her.

Why hadn't he sorted out the thermostat so that the heating came on? They weren't that skint.

Clare pulled on her jeans again without getting out from beneath the duvet and it was as she was doing this that she noticed that the room didn't look quite the same as usual. For a start, it was tidy. There was not a solitary sock to be seen on Daniel's side of the room, which usually looked like an explosion in a Chinese laundry. Something else was odd too ... The walls, usually graced with three paintings Daniel had done when they first arrived in Cornwall, were bare.

'My God, we've been burgled,' was Clare's first thought as she leapt out of bed and ran through into the lounge. But nothing had changed there. And Daniel's painting rucksack was still lying on the kitchen table, so he hadn't left her. Slowly, Clare pushed open the door to the studio and the mystery was solved. A mattress lay in the middle of the floor, and in the middle of the mattress lay Daniel.

The light which streamed in through the open door awoke him and he looked up to see who was intruding on his sleep, his arm shading his eyes.

'What are you doing in here?' Clare asked.

Daniel didn't answer. He just pulled his sleeping bag tightly up to his chin and rolled over so that he had his back to her.

'Why have you moved all your stuff out of the bedroom?'

'Guess,' he muttered.

'Oh, come on,' Clare groaned. 'You can't be mad at me. I was away for four days, Daniel.'

'Five,' he corrected.

'You've been away for longer than that before . . .'

'Yeah. But with my mates, Clare, and not to Paris. Who did you go with?'

Clare sensed an impending crisis. 'Fran, from school. I told you. You spoke to her on the phone.' A voice inside Clare's head asked her why she was trying to justify the weekend to him. It would be far, far better to try and laugh it off than to get into some deep debate about it that might reveal more than she wanted to.

'And who else?'

'No one else. It was a weekend for two . . . We even had separate beds,' she added with a nervous laugh.

'Yeah.'

'Daniel,' Clare pleaded. She dropped down on to the mattress beside him. His body seemed to mould into hers momentarily before he remembered the new status quo and moved further towards the other side. She laid a hand on his shoulder which he quickly pushed away. Clare struggled to contain her frustration. She had thought everything over while she was away and had arrived back in Cornwall longing to see Daniel, to hold him and get things back to how they once were. Now he seemed determined to make things worse.

'Oh, for God's sake, Daniel,' she snapped suddenly, 'stop acting like a spoilt child over this. I needed the break. I deserved the break.'

'And I didn't.' Daniel rolled over so that his steely eyes locked hers. His brows were knitted together in a frown that she had never seen before. 'I thought we were meant to be together forever, Clare. In Lurve,' he mocked the word. 'And then you go off to Paris with some girl that you haven't bothered to keep in touch with for five or so years, to spend a weekend shagging frogs.'

'Daniel, that's not fair!'

'Isn't it? Go and listen to the message you left.'

Clare jumped to her feet and then hesitated. If she was innocent, as she claimed to be, she wouldn't be bothered about what the message said. What had she said? She tried to remember. Daniel had saved the messages. Clare pressed 'play'. Her mother, ringing to ask how she was getting on. Daniel's friend Gary. Then her voice. Clare calling to say that she wouldn't be home.

In the background, Francesca's tinkling laugh. A phrase in French. Incomprehensible, but definitely male. It wasn't even Jean.

Daniel had dragged himself out of bed and now stood at the door to the studio, the sleeping bag draped around his shoulders like a child's attempt to simulate a batman cape. 'Well,' he said, his eyes narrowing accusingly.

Clare's shoulders, which had been tensing up as they rowed so that it hurt to move, now suddenly began to release again.

'It was nothing,' she said, thinking quickly. 'Fran had a friend in Paris, called Bertrand. Her brother's pen-pal I think. He just came up to our room for a coffee. Just to be friendly. He wasn't even as handsome as Fran remembered him to be . . .' Clare hoped that detail had sounded light. 'And he definitely wasn't anywhere near as handsome and gorgeous as you.' She took a risk and fluttered her eyelashes at him.

Daniel's face was softening.

'Really?' he asked.

'Yes, really.' Clare felt her voice wobble. 'He was the only man I spoke to all weekend.'

'God. I don't know what's wrong with me,' Daniel said. 'I feel like a fool accusing you like that but you know how much I brood about these things when I'm on my own. And then when I heard his voice . . . It's just that I had such a crap weekend without you here.'

The breath escaped Clare's body like steam from a kettle. He was right next to her now. Dropping the sleeping bag to the floor. His arms wrapping around Clare's shoulders as he whispered an

162

apology into her ear. An apology which turned into the lightest of kisses.

'I love you, Clare, that's all. I can't stand the thought of anyone else being near you. Anyone. Anyone at all. I was even jealous of Fran in case she turned out to be a rabid lesbian . . .'

Clare laughed ironically to herself and kissed Daniel softly on the cheek.

'I love you too,' she told him.

Daniel's hand moved up the back of her neck. He dipped his head to place a kiss on her collar-bone.

'I've missed you, Clare, really missed you,' he murmured. 'Don't ever go away without me again.'

Clare felt a stinging at the back of her eyes. Love, guilt, worry. She gulped down a sob as Daniel continued to kiss his way down her body, carefully unbuttoning her thick cotton pyjama shirt. She shut her eyes tightly to stop the tears from escaping as his hands slid smoothly across her bare skin to rest on either side of her waist.

But Daniel saw that her eyelashes had become wet and transferred his attention to her unhappy eyes. He let his lips rest first on one closed lid and then on the other, sipping away her tears. Clare's arms, which had been hanging loosely at her sides, now came up to rest around his neck and her lips finally sought his.

The way he held her intensified the thoughts that were racing through her mind. How could she have done it? How could she have been unfaithful to this dear man? This man whose touch could still excite her and was even now beginning to make her feel the urge to grind her hips against his, and pull his body right into her heart.

Playfully, Daniel took Clare in a dancing hold, one arm around her back, the other holding her right hand high. 'One, two, three, one, two, three.' They waltzed into the bedroom. His playfulness brought a smile to her now hopelessly tearful face as he waltzed her right up to the edge of the bed and tipped her backwards on to it.

'Are you OK?' he asked, licking a tear away. 'I've had my tantrum. Everything's fine now.'

Clare nodded. 'Yes. Come here.' She pulled his head down so that his lips met hers. Her tongue teased his teeth apart and she explored the inside of his mouth, tickling and tantalising him.

'I love the way you kiss,' he murmured. He undid the only button which was still fastened and slipped her shirt off her shoulders. Clare wriggled her arms until she was totally free of its restraint, then she reached up and helped to ease Daniel out of his tight white T-shirt. Naked from the waist up, they lay together and continued to kiss for a while. Clare's hands thrilled to the touch of the skin on his back. Smooth and dry. Better than silk.

'I want to make love to you,' he told her. She answered him with the lightest of pinches on his left buttock. Her fingers slipped beneath the edges of the legs of his tight-fitting shorts. She knew he liked that. The feeling of her hands breaching his underwear. His skin was somehow more sensitive at the boundary of being clothed and being naked.

He writhed appreciatively.

He pulled himself up and knelt between her

thighs. He studied her half naked body, prone on the bed, then took a breast in each hand and massaged them slowly, gently. Her nipples hardened as if to command. She trailed her own hands down his chest, her long fingers catching in the light layer of dark hair. She reached his well-muscled abdomen. Played like a xylophone the six muscles that he had worked so hard on and that she was always pleased to see. Her finger circled his deep belly button.

Daniel was echoing her movements. Sweeping his fingers down over her slender torso. Then he stopped and just gazed silently at the body before him. The pale white skin that he loved so much, though he always teased her about her inability to go brown in the sun. Her breasts, just the right size, though he always teased her about them being a little small. Her delicate collar-bone. Her perfect waist. How was she to know that he loved her? He had never really told her often enough.

'I love you,' he murmured now. 'I love you, I love you.' He had said it more times that day than in the whole time they had been together.

The back of Clare's throat prickled to hear it, prickled with the gathering of yet more tears.

'Don't be sad,' he told her, seeing the clouds gathering in her eyes. Secretly he felt glad that he seemed to be having such a strong effect on her emotions. He leaned over her and found her mouth again. Clare kissed him gratefully, grateful to be able to divert his attention from her eyes.

Her fingers found the elastic of his shorts again and this time she tugged them down. His penis, already hard, escaped its cotton confines and now hovered between them. Still echoing her movements, his fingers made short work of the silver buttons on her jeans and they joined his shorts on the floor.

Clare wrapped her fingers around his shaft and coaxed it into maximum stiffness. He fumbled through her pubic hair to find her waiting lips. She was wet; he always made her wet, even when she thought she didn't want to. An involuntary giggle of pleasure escaped her.

Daniel slowly slid his fingers up and down the delicate contours of her labia. He could feel them slowly swelling, parting, inviting him in. He moved his hand so that the heel of his palm was hard against her clitoris, and increased the pressure there while the fingers lay still in her shiny vulva. Clare moved her body upwards, trying to drive him inside. His other hand slipped beneath her and wandered lazily over the firm curve of her buttocks.

Clare sought his lips to kiss him but he moved his head away, kissing instead down the side of her neck. A gentle nip from his teeth made her tense with anticipation. With his hand at her sex and his lips at her neck, she felt as though her body was an elastic band, stretched out to its fullest length, waiting hopefully to be allowed to spring free. Her breath vibrated through her aching body. She was so incredibly aware of everything at that moment, of the hairs raised by goosebumps along the length of her trembling thighs, of the swelling of her crimson lips, the dilation of her pupils, the hardening of her nipples. Her body was literally growing towards him.

Daniel pushed a single finger into her. Clare's back arched, captured by this small invasion. She moaned his name and it came out like a sigh.

'Daniel.'

He was sitting astride her legs now. Through narrowed eyes she saw his penis bob with excitement as her body bucked toward him again.

'I love you,' he told her once more. He had withdrawn his hand, his fingers shiny with her wetness. He licked them clean, enjoying the way she still blushed slightly at the sight of his petty debauchery.

'Move up the bed,' he whispered.

Clare shuffled herself backwards with her hips until her head almost touched the headboard. She reached her hands behind her and took hold of the twisted metal arc. The sunray of black tubing was awful, but it served its purpose. Clare knew that she was striking Daniel's favourite pose. She drew her legs up automatically. One on either side of his body. He ran his hands up her calves and lowered himself into position.

Clare released one hand from the headboard and stroked the approaching penis lovingly. Enticingly. Daniel focused on the silky triangle of dark hair at the top of her thighs. He curved his hips. Clare lifted her head so that one of his arms could curl around her neck. He still needed the other hand to guide himself inside.

They groaned simultaneously. Daniel waited patiently while Clare adjusted her position minutely so that any pain was instantly pleasure.

His lips fell on her forehead and tasted the salt of her sweat. Her hot hands closed on his buttocks.

Daniel began to glide in and out of her. Like a well-oiled machine. Noiselessly at first, except for the tiny sounds of sweat on sweat. Then breathing more audibly as he increased his pace. Clare's mouth had opened. Her lips curved into a helpless smile.

'Faster, faster,' she murmured like a mantra.

He did as he was told.

Daniel raised himself up on his arms. Straightening them until the joints locked and he could hold himself there without effort. He looked down at the junction between their bodies. They were polished with sweat. Her breasts perfectly rounded. His muscles defined by the exertion as though they were cut from stone.

Clare gazed at the point where he went into her. On the upstroke, his penis appeared miraculously from the centre of her pubic hair, oiled with her pleasure. The veins stood up all along it. It was so hard. Impossible to imagine that it wasn't always like that.

In, in, in. The sight of his penetration heightened the sensation. Her vagina sang with the friction. She heard the quickening of his breath that meant he was just about to come but instead he slowed right down. Counting to himself. Thinking about the sea. He withdrew almost the entire length. The head of his penis hovered between her labia.

She hated it when he did that, hated it and loved it all at the same time. That upstroke seemed to take forever. An agony like the slow separation of a sticking plaster from your skin.

'Daniel!' she squealed. She grasped his buttocks and forced him back inside. His arms buckled beneath him and he collapsed down on to her chest. His pelvis had already taken over. Thrusting, thrusting, thrusting. Clare's rhythmic moan began to rise and rise in pitch.

'Oh, now,' she mumbled. 'Now, Daniel, come now.'

His eyes were screwed tightly shut.

She used his buttocks to help pump his pelvis against her pubic bone. To speed him up to the optimum. To bring his orgasm crashing into her. She tensed her legs against the bed. Raised her pelvis to his again and again.

'Oh, God. No, no,' she cried.

Daniel buried his face in the pillow beside her head while his loins jerked against her. His muffled moans spurred her own end on. She wrapped her legs around his back and held him captive until the sperm began to dribble out down her thighs.

The sheet beneath them was sodden with sperm, sweat and now, as they lay quietly side by side, Daniel's tears.

'Daniel,' Clare said later, as they were sitting in front of the television, picking at a late breakfast of two slices of toast made from the only remaining bread in the house, 'we really do have to sort a few things out.'

The exhilaration, the tenderness of their lovemaking was slowly fading again. An advert for EuroDisney came on screen and Clare could see Daniel's expression blacken at this reminder of her weekend in France. Had he really believed her, or was he, like her, pretending that nothing had happened, because it was easier tht way?

'Yeah,' he said flatly.

Daniel moved his things back into the bedroom. Clare was relieved to see the red and yellow paintings back on the wall, though in the past they had occasionally been too much for her when she awoke hungover. She straightened the middle one as she passed it.

For the first time since returning from France, Clare wandered into the studio with the intention of picking up her brushes and adding something to the portrait of Steve. She pulled away the sheet that covered it and looked at the painting with a critical eye. The form was there. The composition was good, but still it wasn't quite right. She tapped the end of a brush against her teeth. There was no life in it.

As she pondered her next move, she was aware of someone behind her. Daniel placed his hands on her shoulders and took his own look at the painting. 'Needs more pink,' he said sarcastically. 'And talking of pink, I saw Francesca when I popped out to get the milk. She's got some things to do in town but then, she says, she's coming round. She can't wait to see you.' He parodied her voice. 'So you better make yourself look pretty.'

Daniel left her alone again. He hadn't sounded too impressed. Why had he said she should make herself look pretty for the visit? Clare remembered the tinkling laugh in the background of her answermachine message. But surely that recorded giggle hadn't been recognisable?

'You left these,' Francesca tipped a pair of earrings into Clare's hand. Clare shoved them into her pocket with a warning look in her eyes, but it was too late, Daniel's eye had been caught by the gesture and he was now fully tuned in to their conversation.

'Daniel tells me you've been away,' Francesca said theatrically.

'Yes,' replied Clare, 'To Paris. With a friend from school – she won some tickets in a competition.'

'Oh, how lucky. It's lovely at this time of year,' said Francesca. 'But I do hope that doesn't mean that you've been getting behind with the painting. I need it finished by the fifteenth, remember.'

'Easily.'

'Can I see it?' Francesca coyly twirled a strand of hair that had escaped from her neat chignon.

'Of course.'

Clare led Francesca into the studio. Daniel watched approvingly as the blonde girl's slim legs passed by on their high heels. Once safely inside, Clare pushed the door to. Francesca immediately took her lover's face in her hands and planted a kiss on her lips.

'Don't,' said Clare, weakly pushing her away. 'Not now.'

'When? When?'

They heard the scraping of a chair as Daniel got up in the other room.

'I'm going to get some bread,' he called.

'Now?' came the answer to Francesca's question.

Francesca brought Clare's lips smacking back down on to her own. Clare struggled vainly to resist the embrace, fight the tongue which, as usual, wanted to gain entry beyond her tightly shut lips.

'Kiss me, idiot,' Francesca demanded.

Their tongues wrestled. Francesca's hands covered her lover's body. Taking in the shape of her through her thin cotton shirt and figure-hugging jeans.

'I like you in this colour,' Francesca murmured as she began to lift the shirt out of the way. Clare tried to suppress a laugh.

'Have you missed me?'

'Of course.'

A cold hand slipped between Clare's shirt and her skin. She shivered pleasurably and responded by hugging Francesca tighter. The fingers spread out across her back, then moved around to the front. They found a delicate nipple, and brought it to stiffness with a combination of icy flesh and warm feelings.

Francesca slipped her head beneath the covering fabric and kissed the hardened bud. Clare moaned softly and clasped Francesca's head appreciatively in her hand. When Francesca emerged her hair was dishevelled, single strands standing on end as a result of the static electricity she was creating.

All too quickly they heard the rattle of the lock and the door creak open again. Daniel whistled his way into the house, as if he knew he was interrupting something and wanted to make sure that he didn't actually walk in on it. Francesca began to talk animatedly about paint textures and canvas weights as if she knew what she was talking about. All the time she stood behind Clare, her head on Clare's shoulder, holding a milky white breast in each of her hands. Clare pushed her bottom backwards so that it rested against Francesca's pelvis, and rotated her buttocks gently. Her hands slid down the tailored skirt that covered Francesca's carefully maintained thighs.

'Coffee? Tea? Me?' Daniel was right outside the door. The girls sprang apart as he slowly pushed his way backwards into the room with a tray in his hands. He handed them their drinks and stood with them, discussing the merits of some artist's use of light and shade. He showed no sign of leaving them again. Indeed, Clare thought that she saw a peculiar look of pleasure gather in his eyes as the conversation began to falter.

After a while, Francesca simply had to go. She gave Clare a cursory, polite society kiss at the door and promised to phone. By the time Clare returned to the sitting-room, Daniel had reinstalled himself on the sofa. Clare looked at him askance as she crossed the room to the studio. Her skin was still warm from Francesca's touch.

# Chapter Fourteen

*CLARE SPENT THE* next short day down by the harbour again, absently running off three more paintings for Graham. These watercolours were coming more and more easily to her and she finished them in less than two hours. On her way back to the flat she stopped at a bakery and bought two éclairs.

It was almost dark as she opened the rusty gate. No lights were on in their flat. Clare thought nothing of it, but was a little disappointed that she would have to wait to eat her éclair. Perhaps she would eat hers straight away anyway. Whistling, she pushed open the door, turned on the light, tossed the pastries on to the table and made straight for the studio to put her painting gear away.

There was an ominous crunching sound as she opened this door with her hip. Something must have fallen against the other side. She flicked the light switch with her elbow, and the sight which greeted her this time rooted her to the spot.

A torn canvas was scattered around the floor of the studio. Which one was it? Clare dropped her bag and picked up a couple of the pieces. Immediately she recognised the portrait of Steve. Cut to shreds. And it looked as if it had been treated to the addition of a few big splodges of black paint first.

'Daniel!' Clare cried angrily. What had he done that for?

Fuming, she stormed back into the kitchen to pick up one of the kitchen knives to treat him to a taste of his own medicine by slashing one of his own precious works. The cutlery drawer opened without its usual rattle. There was nothing in it. She opened the crockery cupboard. That too was empty. Had they been burgled?

Confused, Clare raced to the bedroom. His paintings were gone again. And the lava lamp that stood by their bed. She flung open the wardrobe. His side was empty.

'Daniel!' she screamed. This time she didn't expect an answer. They hadn't been burgled. Daniel had gone. He had taken his things and left.

Clare dropped the fragment of Steve's portrait which she still clutched in her sweating hand back on to the floor.

She searched the flat from top to bottom for some kind of explanation, a letter or a note, but there was none. He hadn't left any forwarding address either, or a number to contact him on. He'd left nothing, nothing at all. Taken everything he owned so that he had no reason to come to the flat again.

'I can't believe it,' Clare said to the bare walls. And all this after she had decided that the game was through and that she loved Daniel as she had always done after all. Why had he left so suddenly? She just couldn't understand it. When she had walked out of the flat that morning he had kissed her goodbye, the same as always. They hadn't even rowed the night before. He must have found out about her affair. Why else would he have ruined the picture of Steve when there were other paintings of which she was infinitely fonder?

She spent that day, and the cold night that followed it, sitting on the sofa – one of the few things Daniel had left behind in the flat – waiting for the phone to ring. She longed to hear her lover's voice – not Daniel's but Francesca's. She had tried dialling her number several times that day only to be confronted by an answermachine. Finally her dialling was met with a human response.

'Hello.' The woman who answered the phone sounded older.

'Hi,' Clare replied. Holding the phone with tight fingers. Waiting for the bomb to drop. 'Is Francesca there?'

'She is, yes. But she doesn't want to speak to anyone at the moment.'

Clare's heart pounded within her rib-cage. Why didn't she want to speak to anyone? Clare forced herself to ask, 'She isn't ill, is she?'

'No,' said the older woman flatly, 'but she has had a bit of a shock.'

'A shock.'

'Yes.' The woman wasn't about to elaborate.

A shock could be one of two things, Clare guessed. Either someone in Francesca's family had died, or she had found out that her husband had been having an affair. The woman on the phone sounded tight-lipped as opposed to distraught.

Francesca had definitely found out about Steve.

'Who's calling please? I'll ask her to call you back when she's feeling a little better . . .'

'It's just a friend. I'll call her back. Goodbye.' Clare cut off the woman by pressing the button on the phone as if putting the receiver down wouldn't have been quick enough. She slumped into the sofa and stared at a fragment of the portrait of Steve she had salvaged from the studio floor.

How had they found out? How had Daniel and Francesca found out about her affair with Steve? She hadn't been to bed with him since returning from Paris and before then she had been discreet, hadn't she? Of course she had. They had only been to bed together three times in all. He had never been to the flat, or phoned her there. They had never been seen in public together . . .

Clare threw the fragment of canvas to the floor.

Except for once.

At Graham's party.

Graham had seen them laughing together and he had seen them leave together. He had quizzed her about it when she took the nude into the gallery two days later. Clare remembered the conversation she and Graham had had about

Steve and Francesca. The distant look in his eyes every time he mentioned Francesca's name. The very fact that Graham had sent Francesca to Clare to have the portrait painting was just a way for him to warn Clare off. Graham was in love with Francesca. He had every reason to tell her that her husband was being unfaithful if he thought that it might drive Francesca into his arms.

Clare snatched up her coat and headed for the door. But what reason did he have to involve her in his revenge plot as well? He must have told Daniel. Clare whirled through the streets of the little fishing town like a hurricane bent on pulling up every tree and house in its path until she reached the door of the Dragon Gallery and pushed it open so hard that it bounced back off the wall.

'Hey, careful!' Graham was sitting at the front desk as usual. His eyes widened in horror at the spectacle of the expensive frosted-glass door ricocheting off the stoppers designed to stop it from smashing. Clare stood in the doorway, her beautiful face screwed up in anger.

'Who nicked your rattle?' he asked her sarcastically. She didn't break into her usual smile.

'Can you shut the shop and come into the back room with me, please?' Clare was so worked up that she could hardly speak her request.

'Oo-er,' Graham gave his standard response, eliciting this time not a standard grimace from Clare but a standard, stinging slap across his stubbly cheek. Graham stumbled backwards in shock. 'What have I done?'

'That's exactly what I want to ask you myself.' Clare flipped the sign on the shop door to 'closed' and ushered Graham through to the back. A customer, alerted to the excitement by the sound of Clare's hand making contact with Graham's floppy jowl, took a break from studying the paintings to see the performance art instead. But Clare gave the customer a nasty, narrow-eyed smile which sent him scuttling straight out of the gallery at top speed.

Graham put on the brakes and grabbed Clare by the top of her arms.

'What on earth do you think you are doing?' he shouted at her. If Graham had been surprised by Clare's sudden show of aggression, she was certainly surprised by the way he had suddenly decided to take matters in hand. 'What is the matter with you?' This question was softer. 'Clare, what on earth can have happened?'

'Oh, for God's sake, Graham. Don't pretend that you don't know. I get home to find that my boyfriend has left me and then when I phone Francesca, she refuses to talk to me—'

Francesca's name sent him into defence.

'Francesca?'

'Yes, Francesca. You know her. Steve's wife. Why did you have to tell her, Graham?'

'Tell her what?'

'Tell her what?!' Clare mimicked. 'About the affair, for God's sake!' She was no longer aggressive, but desperate, her shoulders shaking as she sobbed. Graham still held the tops of her arms. Clare tried listlessly to push his hands away.

'The affair?' Graham looked at her curiously. 'Explain.'

'Steve's affair,' Clare spat.

Graham's face retained an air of puzzlement. 'I had to, Clare. I love Francesca, I didn't want her to get hurt by that bastard husband of hers . . . But, but I don't see why it should have anything to do with you?'

'What do you mean "you don't see why it should have anything to do with me"?' Her eyes flashed with anger again. 'You told Daniel as well that I was having an affair with Steve, didn't you?'

'I . . .' Graham released Clare's shoulders and sat down on the edge of his desk. His eyes bored into her face, demanding an explanation from her. 'You?' he said incredulously. 'You were having an affair with Steve?'

The look which now passed across Graham's face threw Clare into confusion. He was acting like he didn't know. No, he wasn't acting. He genuinely didn't know.

'Yes. Well, no. Not really an affair. I just saw him a few times after your party.'

'Oh, God.' Graham scrunched up as much hair as he could find on his head in his hands. 'Oh God, Clare. What a mess this is. What a mess!' The tears were streaming down her face as she tried to comprehend what Graham was trying to let her know.

'I didn't know, Clare. I didn't say anything to Daniel about you and Steve. I didn't think you would get mixed up with someone like him. What did Daniel say?'

'Nothing.' Clare spluttered. 'He didn't leave a note or anything. It's just . . .' She sniffed loudly. 'All his things have gone from the flat and he ripped the painting I was doing of Steve to pieces . . .'

'I didn't tell him, I promise.'

'But why did he ruin the painting of Steve? He must have known. What did you tell Francesca? Why won't she come to the phone?'

'I told Francesca everything that I knew,' Graham continued. 'That Steve has been having an affair with my wife.'

'Your wife?'

'Yes. Apparently so.'

'Oh, God,' Clare threw her arms around the narrow shoulders of the man she had despised seconds before and they clung to each other for support. When they had calmed down a little, Graham dashed out into the front of the shop and locked the front door. He made tea, still sniffing. He had never cried before. Let alone in front of a girl.

'I wrote her a letter,' Graham explained. 'But I didn't sign it, or say who was involved, of course, because my wife and Francesca were supposed to be friends.'

'Graham,' Clare looked at him with sad eyes. 'I don't know what to say. You must feel so hurt. Your wife . . .'

'Oh, it was all over between us years ago. In fact, it was probably even over before it began. I was always in love with Francesca, who never even noticed me, and Jackie was just in love with my money. Or the money she thought I had. She

181

was completely furious when I bought this gallery. Said we would lose all our money and that's when I realised that she didn't love me. She wasn't happy with the idea that having a gallery would make *me* happy . . . She's had affairs before but I was surprised to walk in on her and Steve . . . To be perfectly honest I thought she was a bit too old for his current tastes. But I guess he had you to satisfy those.'

Clare snorted indignantly. 'I can't believe I was taken in.'

'He takes everyone in, Clare.'

'But I don't understand why Daniel would have gone and why he would have ripped up that painting first . . .'

'Perhaps, perhaps he just sensed that it was something you were proud of. Perhaps he was going to go away anyway. He never seemed to be totally at home here . . .' Clare nodded gravely. She knew that Graham was right. 'And his pictures of boats were simply terrible.'

At that Clare couldn't help laughing out loud.

As Clare left the gallery and began the walk back to her flat, she wouldn't have said that she felt happy exactly but she certainly felt different. The gulls screeching overhead drew her eyes upwards. She smiled faintly at the winter blue sky, and breathed in the salt-scented air. St Ives hadn't been their dream, it had been her dream. A romantic idyll which suffocated Daniel and perhaps had begun to suffocate her.

Walking down the narrow cobbled street she began to notice for the first time the cracks in her vision. The plastic flowers in the hanging baskets, the net curtains, the Cornish piskies straight from Taiwan. Perhaps she needed to move on as well. She looked out across the sea. She'd used this place up. She remembered a different view. From Jean's room.

Since Daniel's sudden disappearance, Clare had set the answermachine to audible alert so that she wouldn't miss a message if he ever tried to call. When she opened the door to the flat, her ears were assailed for the first time by the high-pitched beep. She rushed to the machine and pressed play, without taking off her coat, without shutting the door.

'Hi, Clare,' came a familiar voice, 'this is Francesca. Mum said someone called – was it you? I need to chat. Don't really want to speak over the phone. I'll be down later today. Be in . . .'

Clare played the message again. When had she left it? How long did Clare have before she arrived on the doorstep? The ringing of the doorbell answered her question.

'Clare!' Francesca fell into her arms. Clare held her tightly and brought her inside. 'Clare. Everything's been so terrible this last week.'

The story tumbled out and Clare couldn't help remembering the first time Francesca had cried in her arms. The letter had arrived the day after they had last been together, Francesca gabbled between sniffs. It wasn't signed, but the postmark was Cornwall and it said that Steven had been having an affair there while working on the new flats.

'It didn't even say who he'd been having an affair with,' Francesca continued, wide-eyed and vulnerable. 'So for all I know I could have passed her in the street on my way here . . .'

Clare shivered at the venom in her voice.

'But I thought you always suspected him of it. I don't see why you're so upset.'

'I didn't really ever think he would,' Francesca sniffed. 'I always said it, but I was only joking. He always said he was too tired to sleep with me after working such long hours down here. I didn't think he'd have the energy to find someone else. Oh, God. I was just stupid. He had all the opportunity he wanted to play around.'

Clare searched the tear-stained face for a trace of the strong, outrageous Francesca who had taken her to Paris. She wasn't there. Instead, sitting on the sofa was the girl Clare had first taken Francesca for, defining herself by her husband.

'It's changed in here,' Francesca said suddenly, blinking her big wet eyes.

'Yes,' Clare replied softly, 'Daniel's gone.'

'Gone?'

'Things weren't working out,' she said cryptically, trying not to let any pain cross her eyes. 'But look, who cares? In fact I'm glad he's gone, because now you're here and you can leave your ratbag husband and come and live with me.'

'No,' Francesca shook her head, her eye brimming again. 'That's why I had to see you. I've talked to Steven about the whole affair. He says it was just something he did while I was in Paris. He was drunk. She was drunk – and it will never

184

happen again. We're going to try again with our marriage. Really try. Spend more time together. Make it work.'

'Make it work?' Clare was incredulous. 'He's a worthless—'

'Sssh,' Francesca put her finger to Clare's lips. 'He's my husband, Clare. I can't just give up. After all, it's not as if I've been exactly faithful, is it?' She laughed – a little nervously, Clare thought. 'But I'm going to be now. That's why I'm here, to tell you that we can't carry on like before. We've got to just be friends now.'

'Friends?'

'Yes. Oh, come on, Clare,' Francesca took Clare's sad face in her hands. 'It couldn't have worked out anyway. I mean, look at us! For a start, we're both girls!'

'Ha ha.'

'Things won't really change that much. We'll still see each other . . . through perhaps not quite so much. We shouldn't have done anything in the first place.'

'Francesca, it's not that. It's not physical, not sex. I just can't believe that you're being taken in by him. He doesn't make you happy. He's not going to stop having affairs.'

'He says that this is the first time he has ever been unfaith—'

'The first time? Who is he kidding?' Clare almost screamed. It was becoming harder and harder to wrestle with the temptation to let her have the truth.

'I want to believe him, Clare.' Francesca was suddenly firm again. 'I'll call you.' She rose from the sofa without any of the usual lingering caresses that preceded her goodbyes and walked purposefully to the door. She stood silently as she waited for Clare to let her out. 'I will phone,' she promised.

Clare closed the door behind her.

Two days later, Francesca did call. She sounded happy, too happy, and babbled on about the preparations for Steven's birthday party as if the girl on the other end of the phone was her grandmother and not her ex-lover. Suddenly she asked, 'You will finish the painting won't you?' Clare hadn't told her that Daniel had already finished it off in his special way. 'I want you to finish it,' Francesca added, after a disconcerting moment of silence.

'Yes,' said Clare, 'I will.'

'And,' Francesca took a deep breath, 'I'd like you to come to the party yourself. To deliver the painting in person.'

'I don't think I . . .'

'It's important to me. I want you to meet Steven. You'll be charmed, I promise . . . Oh, Clare, yesterday, when I got home from the gym there were two hundred roses in the hallway! Well, I nearly sneezed myself to death, but the thought! And then . . .'

Clare listened to Francesca's excited babbling without hearing. This wasn't the girl she knew at all. Perhaps she should just let her go. Let her find out in a year or two years that while a snake can shed its skin, it can never alter its fundamental nature.

'So you'll come to the party?'

Clare's attention had drifted to the pile of dirty crockery that stood by the sink.

'Clare, you'll come to the party, won't you?'

'It's such a long way to come. And I won't know anyone.'

'You know me . . . I'll introduce you to some nice bloke.'

'You've swung it.' Clare forced a laugh.

She decided to go for a walk by the sea to clear her head and make some decisions. The beauty of the moon reflected in the sea didn't thrill her that night. She just felt loss. Only a week earlier she had been panicking in the face of too much love. How different things were now.

Francesca was going to give her marriage another chance. Perhaps she wasn't wrong to do that. As she herself had said, the infidelity hadn't exactly been one-sided. She obviously loved Steve. Another part of Clare's mind protested that Francesca was just scared of being alone, scared of losing her stability and respectability. She could only swing with no knickers on the flying trapeze if she had a safety net to fall into.

'Hmm.' Clare let the wind play over her hair. She didn't care. She didn't care about any of them. She could live without them all. After all, a month ago she hadn't even met them. Well, she hadn't met Francesca and Steve. Daniel was another matter entirely. The hole left by four years with him was probably only just beginning to open. She let her knees fold beneath her and sat down. Her skirt spread out around her, like a beached jellyfish floating down on to the sand. Clare was so absorbed by the question of what she should do next that she didn't notice the figure of a man walking in her direction along the black water's edge until he was almost level with her. The figure gave a casual wave.

Clare looked up when the movement caught her attention.

It was Steve.

Strolling towards her in his designer jacket and jeans like the proverbial bad penny.

'Well met by moonlight,' he called as he neared her. 'Fancy meeting you here.'

'You said that last time,' Clare replied wearily.

'Mind if I join you?'

'I'd rather you didn't.'

'How was Paris?'

'Different.'

He had ignored her request to be alone and sat down beside her, picking up handfuls of sand and letting the grains run out through his open fingers. Clare watched his beautiful hands, remembered involuntarily what he could do with them, and then tried not to think about it.

'I was having a drink in the bar up there,' he motioned to the hotel which overlooked the bay. 'I saw your silhouette in the moonlight, recognised you by the way you walk. Couldn't believe my luck. I didn't think I'd ever see you again.'

'Likewise,' Clare huffed in reply.

'I love it down here,' he continued regardless. 'Can't imagine walking by the Thames like this, can you?'

Clare didn't answer.

'I wish I could stay here forever, but the project will be finished next week and then I suppose I will have to go back to London and frighten my tenants there . . . This place is like paradise.'

Clare would have agreed. She gazed stonily at the sand in front of her feet.

'What's the matter with you?' he asked. 'Aren't we friends anymore?'

Friends? Had they ever been friends?

'I just want to be on my own, Steve, that's all.'

It wasn't the answer he wanted. He gave up dribbling the grains of sand back on to the beach and instead dropped a few of them on to her shoe. Clare flicked them off in irritation. Steve replaced them with another handful.

'Will you stop that?' she hissed. She rose to her feet and started to walk back up the beach, the sand keeping her from going quite as quickly as she wanted to.

Steve followed close behind.

'I love it when you're angry,' he told her.

'Oh, you really haven't seen me angry,' Clare warned him.

'What's wrong, Clare? When you left for Paris I thought we were getting on really well. I've been praying that we'd bump into each other again . . .'

Clare tried not to listen. She focused on the reflection of the moon in the waves. This was the man that Francesca was trying to rescue her marriage with. Suddenly his hand grasped her arm.

'Let go.' She tried to shake him free.

He whirled her around to face him, forced her close to him and kissed her protesting lips. He didn't loosen his grip on her until he felt her soften beneath his kiss, felt her lips give way and part. He held her tightly until her angry eyes started to close.

'Don't tell me you haven't thought about me at all . . .' he murmured into her reddening cheek.

Not in the way you think, Clare wanted to say, but she held back. Deep inside, part of her still wanted to see just how far the reformed Steve would go.

His hand moved languorously in the long hair which tumbled down her back. It was knotted by the wind. Occasionally his fingers found the knots and it hurt.

'I've dreamed about your body in the moonlight.' His voice caressed her far more subtly than his hands. 'Your porcelain skin and that beautiful mahogany hair.'

'You make me sound like a piece of furniture,' Clare snorted, fighting his determination to break her resolve.

'All the time I find myself thinking about the way you looked when you were standing at the window on that first evening we spent together. Wearing that red dress. The white curtains billowing around you. The smile in your eyes.'

He kissed her closed eyelids and Clare remembered the first time as well. She remembered his smile.

'Your nipples, showing pink through your white camisole . . .'

He pulled her body closer still to his own. Her arms had nowhere to go but around his back. She breathed him in, the smell of him clouding the anger she had been carrying in her mind, breaking her down like a slow poison. His hand rested on her buttocks, pulled her pelvis towards his. She felt his stiffening dick.

He began to kiss her again. This time her tongue tangled with his. He moaned his pleasure at her silent acquiescence before leaving her mouth to move his lips along the length of her neck. He held her hair up and out of the way. It was like a tent, concealing his furtive worship from the empty beach.

'I can't,' she said suddenly, pushing him away ineffectually with her chilly hands.

'Ssssh.' He kissed her as though his lips were a pacifier. He was using the gentle weight of his body against hers to move her backwards up the sand. Soon they were in the shade of the sea wall. The golden sand on to which they sank was night black.

'Stop,' she said – pleaded.

His hand moved to the front of her body, sliding up and down her breasts, computing the easiest way inside her blouse. The buttons were at the back so the hand untucked her shirt from the waistband and slid beneath it.

The coolness of his fingers against her uncovered belly made her draw in her breath. Their chill was quickly abated as he flattened the hand out, stealing the warmth from her blood. His lips still pressed hers urgently, preventing any more protestations. Her returning kisses defied her brain.

The hand beneath her shirt found a breast and then a nipple. He rolled the nipple between his fingers, beginning to make the soft animal noises of plesaure that he had made when first discovering her body. He writhed impatiently, grinding his pelvis against nowhere in particular, then pushing her over on to her back and lying full length on top of her. She could feel his penis hard against her thigh. He shifted so that it lay between her legs. They parted a little wider to let him comfortably inside.

Her eyes started to sting with tears that he wouldn't be able to see. Her body was responding like a traitor to his overtures, swelling, hardening and moistening to complement his. As he ground his denim-clad pelvis ever harder against hers, which was covered only by thin layers of pretty ethnic print, she could not cut out the fantastic sensation of the friction in her clitoris. Her nipples burned beneath his tongue as he pushed her top out of the way. The breeze coming in from the sea couldn't keep her skin cool now.

As he sucked her nipple up between his teeth, her fingers began to stroke the tense arc of his neck. Without breaking contact between his tongue and her body for a minute, he shrugged off his jacket. Suddenly, he was more visible. The feeble light of the moon captured and intensified by his billowing white shirt.

Clare arched her back in reply to a line of nipping kisses from her breasts, down her side, to the waistband of her skirt. He gently bit the skin again in the place that had always made her groan loudest.

'No, no.' Her protests were lost in the sound of the water dragging pebbles back into the sea, and her hips raised themselves voluntarily to help him shed her skirt. Her tights were dragged down with it, to her calves, exposing her soft, white thighs. One hand on each, Steve used his grip on her to pull her half on to his knees. Her tights were still in the way. He pulled them fully off and repositioned her. One leg to each side of him. Her bottom on his kneeling thighs. Her pelvis pointing towards heaven and her long hair dragging behind in the cold, dry sand. She let her arms fall backwards above her head. Her body was now in a position of total surrender.

His hands slid up the inside of her thighs until his thumbs rested on either side of her mound. She felt a wave of warmth as he leaned forward over her, his shirt touching her bare, sensitised flesh. He kissed her stretched out belly. Rubbed his face against the downy velvet skin. Peach skin. He was moaning softly just from the pleasure of having her to touch. Clare drew her knees higher and squeezed the body between them. His kiss travelled down her as he curled himself upright again.

Regarding her now from his elevated position, he moved his hands over her like a healer, a magician. Quickly, quickly, up and down and in circles. The friction brought heat to her skin again, made it hum with blood. He woke up nerve endings begging for more. Her pelvis thrust itself further upwards, demanding attention. His hands sought it out. His thumbs carefully parted her lips, bringing a slow smile to his face when he saw how wet they were.

A first finger slipped easily inside. He drew it

out slowly, taking pleasure in the feeling of her and the sound of her taking pleasure from him. She sighed. Her pelvis raised automatically to meet his descending finger again. And again. And again.

He worked his hand faster and faster. Using sometimes two fingers, sometimes three. His other hand concentrated on her clitoris. Pinching it, rubbing it. Her sighs were louder, her hips rolling from side to side as she tried to dodge the very maximum sensation that could send her over the edge. Her backside had slipped off his lap and she was rolling in the sand. Her juices ran down between her buttocks to pick up the tiny grains.

'Fuck me,' she said, hardly recognising the gravelly, urgent voice that escaped her mouth. 'Fuck me now.'

'No,' he told her. 'Not yet.'

He slid backwards in the sand until he was lying face down between her legs. She could feel his hot breath on her inner thighs, the coolness of the evaporating wetness that ran from her vagina. His tongue flickered out to taste, and her muscles tensed at the touch.

'No, no,' she moaned. The battle in her mind was now only serving to heighten the sensation in her body. She could feel the ripples beginning, could hold off no longer. Her body began to shudder uncontrollably in his hands. Her breasts rose and fell with the waves, faster and faster as the ripples descended her thighs. Her breath fluttered out of her body.

'Now, yes?' he asked.

Her sex was suddenly cold in the icy sea air. He

had left off his frantic tonguing and was now positioning himself so that he too got some of the pleasure. Her breath quickened still more in anticipation as he fumbled on the condom, cursing the ubiquitous sand.

'Now, now,' she echoed, lifting her pelvis up to meet his. He cupped her buttocks with one hand and used the other to guide himself in. She exhaled with a loud, resonant sigh as he drove into her. Driving her conscience further from her body with each thrust he made.

She closed her eyes against the shadow of his face and let herself be all touch, all sound. The sea seemed to be getting closer. The wind was rising. He lifted the top half of his body away from her and she felt the cold air rush in between them. He closed the gap again and pumped more furiously. When she cried out in ecstasy, the wind stole her words and they flew out to sea.

Afterwards they lay side by side in the sand. Steve was making a pattern with his right arm like a child in the snow. Clare's head was cradled in the crook of his left. She pulled closer to him and tucked herself into the folds of his shirt for warmth. The animal heat of their love-making all but blown away now.

'Come back to my hotel?' he asked, when the wind began to breech his clothes once more.

'No,' she sniffed. 'I can't.'

'Why not?'

'Why didn't you tell me that you're married, Steve?'

A moment of silence stretched between them.

He cleared his throat.

'Married?' he asked. His voice remained steady, without emotion. 'Because I'm not.'

She didn't bother to present him with the evidence. Instead she got unsteadily to her feet, threw her coat over her shoulder and left, without saying another word. He stayed behind on the sand, watching her until she disappeared into the all-enveloping folds of the black night. He didn't even bother to call her name. Steve had suddenly realised that this particular game was over for him . . . but he would easily find another willing pawn to play by his rules.

The walk back to Clare's flat was cold and long, but it was helpful. By the time she turned her key in the door, she already knew exactly what she had to do.

The new painting was finished. Smiling, Clare wrapped the freshly framed canvas in bubble-wrap to protect the glass as she transported it from Cornwall to London, where Francesca had asked her to attend the party. Clare hadn't been sure at first. She imagined Steve's face when she walked in. Would he show even a spark of recognition for the artist whom he knew so much better than any of the guests would have suspected? Misreading Clare's apprehension, Francesca had assured her that she would not reveal that Clare had been anything other than a painter of pictures to the good lady wife of the subject. Eventually Clare had been persuaded, but, she told Francesca, she would have to turn

196

up a little late. She had things to do in Cornwall and wouldn't be able to get away until at least seven. Francesca begged her to send the picture down ahead, just in case, but Clare refused.

'I might have to tighten the canvas in the frame again before I can let you have it,' she had explained.

'You're a perfectionist,' Francesca laughed affectionately.

'Yeah . . . I just want everything to be exactly right for that special moment,' Clare had cooed into the phone.

Now the day had arrived. Clare covered the layer of bubble-wrap with the paper that Francesca had requested for her husband's gift. It was metallic silver, dotted with tiny red hearts. There was a matching gift-tag on to which Clare had written 'To my darling husband Steve, All my love, Francesca' in her most careful calligraphy. The painting lay on the kitchen table while Clare did the last of her chores before she prepared for the party. As she packed a case, she brought the red silk dress out of her wardrobe and held it up to her body. It had been dry-cleaned twice since Graham's gallery do but the faint trace of spilled punch still showed to knowing eyes. Clare folded the dress carefully over the back of a chair and began to work out how she was going to fit all her shoes into one bag.

Packing finished, the cases all safely stowed in the boot of the car she had hired to drive to the capital, Clare walked up to the flat one last time to dress for the party. She had left her cream silk underwear out of the suitcase as well and now she slipped that on over her perfumed skin. She smoothed it flat across the gentle curve of her belly and her softly swelling hips. The perfect background. It was very, very important that everything was perfect that night. Clare sighed as she rolled the first of her stockings slowly up her leg, stretching it up to meet her suspender belt, remembering other occasions when she had taken this much care to dress. She slipped the red dress over her head and shook out the skirt. She locked eyes with her reflection in the mirror as she decided how she would wear her hair.

'Up, or down?' she asked herself. Crazy, crazy girl, she thought. After all, it wasn't as if anyone would actually see her. She would deliver the picture to the hotel and then leave. And anyway, all those hours ahead in the car would be bound to leave her looking a little the worse for wear. But if something's worth doing . . . Clare twisted her hair into a thick, smooth French pleat.

Francesca fussed nervously around the ballroom where a waiter was laying out the guests' name cards according to her grand plan. Six or seven of them were already in the bar, under the watchful eye of her mother. Steven was somewhere in town with his younger brother, who had promised to keep him out of the way until everyone was assembled to maximise the surprise. As she followed the waiter around, double-checking everything off against her personal lists, Francesca realised with horror that she had seated an elderly aunt next to one of Steven's less discreet builder friends and had to rearrange an entire table to compensate for the blunder. She looked at her watch, surveyed the room. The birthday banner in place above the top table. The candles as yet unlit. The empty easel waiting for the centrepiece of the whole evening to arrive. When would Clare arrive with that damn painting? She should have demanded that it be sent on ahead. Francesca began to chew her lip, tasted lipstick and stopped.

'Is there a phone in here?' she inadvertently snapped at the waiter.

He pointed her in the right direction. Francesca picked up the phone and began to dial Clare's number. Four, one, eight . . . She couldn't remember any more of the number she once knew by heart. She dashed back to her handbag to dig out her address book, flipped to the dog-eared page where the letters of Clare's name had been traced over and over, and started to dial again.

'The number you have dialled has not been recognised,' came the clipped electronic tone. Francesca replaced the receiver and dialled again. More slowly this time. 'The number you have dialled . . .' Click. Where was she? Where was Clare? Francesca punched the number into the phone one last time. 'The number . . .' Francesca chewed an immaculate finger. So her phone was out of order.

'I mustn't panic,' Francesca told herself under her breath.

Clare would be on her way. Of course she would. And now that Francesca thought about it, Clare had said that she might be a little late.

The manager of the hotel sidled up to Francesca

across the shiny parquet floor.

'Mrs Philip?'

'What is it?' Francesca was automatically on guard. She saw the manager's face wince involuntarily at her tone. 'Oh, I'm sorry,' she explained, 'it's just that I want everything to be just right this evening.'

'I understand, madam.'

What he didn't understand was that it was her chance to prove to Steven that he was right to give their marriage another try.

The manager continued in his deferential way, 'I've come to say that the bar is getting a little crowded and so I thought it might be a good idea to begin to move the guests in for dinner.'

'Yes, of course. Do ... do whatever ...' Francesca waved at the room vaguely then she fled to the toilet for one last make-up check before the big moment. Her reflection was comforting. She was wearing Steven's favourite dress, the green one that he had picked out for her during a rare spell of good taste while they were celebrating their first anniversary in Paris. As Francesca brushed a stray hair from her shoulder, she suddenly had a vivid picture of another girl in that dress and it took a few moments before she remembered that she had lent it to Clare. And how much better it had looked with Clare's dark, red streaked hair. She'd taken their split so well ...

'Francesca, there you are.' An older woman's reflection had appeared in the mirror beside the blonde girl. 'Jeremy just telephoned on his mobile to say that he and Steven are almost here.

Everyone is sitting down ready. The manager wants to know whether you want to dim all the lights to the room until Steven walks through the door? I think that's a good idea. Do you think that's a good idea? Do you? Dear?' Francesca's mother laid a comforting hand on her shoulder.

'I'm sorry, Mum,' said Francesca, suddenly smiling again. 'I'm just a bit stressed out with all the arrangements . . . yes, dim the lights. That's the best idea.'

Mother and daughter bustled out into the ballroom again to await the arrival of the man of the moment.


Clare missed her turning on the motorway and had to make a twelve mile detour but she was sure she would still make it to London in plenty of time. The hire car was bigger than any car she had ever driven before – when she put her foot down, it actually made a difference. When she had put her foot down in the car she once shared with Daniel, the only danger she had been in was of her foot going through the rusty floor. The stereo pumped out loud fast music. She opened the window so that the wind whipped loose strands of her hair backwards and forwards across her face. The music was almost drowned out by the sound of the rushing air except for the constant bass beat that raced her heart. The red tarmac of Devon and Cornwall was long behind her. A fine mist of rain made the black bitumen ahead of her shine like patent leather.

The room waited silently in darkness as Steve and

his brother made their approach. Francesca strained to hear their footsteps in the lobby. She twisted her hands together, praying that the portrait would arrive in time. A familiar laugh bellowed out at a bad joke. The double doors swung open and the room was suddenly filled with light.

'Ta-daaa!' Francesca pulled a party pose as her beloved husband stood rooted to the spot in surprise. Her terror subsided when she saw him grin from ear to ear. He drew nearer to her through the gaudily decorated room, shaking the hands of friends and relations as he went. The family man, the trusted friend, the husband whom she loved.

'Thank you, darling,' he murmured as he kissed her. His breath told her that Michael had already plied him with drink. 'How did you get hold of all these people, you clever thing?'

'She went through your little black book,' a red-faced man laughed. Steve blanched at the thought.

'Happy birthday, darling.'

Francesca was handing over a huge, flat parcel, just rushed to the top table by the manager's PA. She was beaming from ear to ear. Clare had made it. Thank heavens. As Steven turned the package over in his hands, making a show of guessing what it was for the other guests, Francesca scanned the back of the room for a sight of her ex-lover. She thought she saw a familiar head of brown hair through the double doors and waved tentatively. Why wasn't Clare coming in?

'Open it, open it,' was the whisper around the

table. Yes, go on Steve, Clare thought as she watched the scene through the tiny window in the door, open the can of worms.

Now Francesca's hands were clasped together in anticipation as he ripped away at the ribbons and tore a strip down the paper to reveal only the back of the picture. It gave away nothing more than the name of an artist that he didn't yet recognise. Finally he shook it free of the paper . . .

'Hold it up, Steve!' called an uncle from the other end of the room. 'Show it to us.'

Steve's face in itself was a picture. As was Francesca's. The beneficent smiles were fading, to be replaced by a look of confusion as the significance of the composition gradually sank in.

'What is it?' a solitary voice called.

Francesca was turning away, her hands to her eyes. Steve held the picture at arm's length.

'Is this a joke?' he asked her, his voice shaking. 'Is this a joke?'

In life-like colours with an ultra-real expression, a lover lay on a bed covered by white cotton sheets. A lover with a serpent, a tattoo from his teens, nestling at the top of a well-muscled thigh.

Clare turned slowly away from the scene. Slowly away from the vision of Francesca running blindly down the centre of the room to the door. Steve calling after her. The laughter of the party guests, unable to see the real joke.

Yes, she thought, her latest nude had been a great success. But the brightly lit room with its exotic human contents held no more inspiration for her now. She closed the hire-car door and checked the glove compartment. Her passport and her one-way ticket. They were still there. Her ticket to Paris, France.

*Already published*

# BACK IN CHARGE
## Mariah Greene

A woman in control. Sexy, successful, sure of herself and of what she wants, Andrea King is an ambitious account handler in a top advertising agency. Life seems sweet, as she heads for promotion and enjoys the attentions of her virile young boyfriend.

But strange things are afoot at the agency. A shake-up is ordered, with the key job of Creative Director in the balance. Andrea has her rivals for the post, but when the chance of winning a major new account presents itself, she will go to any lengths to please her client – and herself . . .

0 7515 1276 1

# THE DISCIPLINE OF PEARLS
## Susan Swann

A mysterious gift, handed to her by a dark and arrogant stranger. Who was he? How did he know so much about her? How did he know her life was crying out for something different? Something . . . exciting, erotic?

The pearl pendant, and the accompanying card bearing an unknown telephone number, propel Marika into a world of uninhibited sexuality, filled with the promise of a desire she had never thought possible. The Discipline of Pearls . . . an exclusive society that speaks to the very core of her sexual being, bringing with it calls to ecstasies she is powerless to ignore, unwilling to resist . . .

0 7515 1277 X

## HOTEL APHRODISIA
**Dorothy Starr**

The luxury hotel of Bouvier Manor nestles near a spring whose mineral water is reputed to have powerful aphrodisiac qualities. Whether this is true or not, Dani Stratton, the hotel's feisty receptionist, finds concentrating on work rather tricky, particularly when the muscularly attractive Mitch is around.

And even as a mysterious consortium threatens to take over the Manor, staff and guests seem quite unable to control their insatiable thirsts . . .

0 7515 1287 7

## AROUSING ANNA
**Nina Sheridan**

Anna had always assumed she was frigid. At least, that's what her husband Paul had always told her – in between telling her to keep still during their weekly fumblings under the covers and playing the field himself during his many business trips.

But one such trip provides the chance that Anna didn't even know she was yearning for. Agreeing to put up a lecturer who is visiting the university where she works, she expects to be host to a dry, elderly academic, and certainly isn't expecting a dashing young Frenchman who immediately speaks to her innermost desires. And, much to her delight and surprise, the vibrant Dominic proves himself able and willing to apply himself to the task of arousing Anna . . .

0 7515 1222 2

# THE WOMEN'S CLUB
**Vanessa Davies**

*Sybarites* is a health club with a difference. Its owner, Julia Marquis, has introduced a full range of services to guarantee complete satisfaction. For after their saunas and facials the exclusively female members can enjoy an 'intimate' massage from one of the club's expert masseurs.

And now, with the arrival of Grant Delaney, it seems the privileged clientele of the women's club will be getting even better value for money. This talented masseur can fulfil any woman's erotic dreams.

Except Julia's . . .

0 7515 1343 1


# PLAYING THE GAME
**Selina Seymour**

Kate has had enough. No longer is she prepared to pander to the whims of lovers who don't love her; no longer will she cater for their desires while neglecting her own.

But in reaching this decision Kate makes a startling discovery: the potency of her sexual urge, now given free rein through her willingness to play men at their own game. And it is an urge that doesn't go unnoticed – whether at her chauvinistic City firm, at the château of a new French client, or in performing the duties of a high-class call girl . . .

0 7515 1189 7

## A SLAVE TO HIS KISS
**Anastasia Dubois**

When her twin sister Cassie goes missing in the South of France, Venetia Fellowes knows she must do everything in her power to find her. But in the dusty village of Valazur, where Cassie was last seen, a strange aura of complicity connects those who knew her, heightened by an atmosphere of unrestrained sexuality.

As her fears for Cassie's safety mount, Venetia turns to the one person who might be able to help: the enigmatic Esteban, a study in sexual mystery whose powerful spell demands the ultimate sacrifice . . .

0 7515 1344 X


## SATURNALIA
**Zara Devereux**

Recently widowed, Heather Logan is concerned about her sex-life. Even when married it was plainly unsatisfactory, and now the prospects for sexual fulfilment look decidedly thin.

After consulting a worldly friend, however, Heather takes his advice and checks in to Tostavyn Grange, a private hotel-cum-therapy centre for sexual inhibition. Heather had been warned about their 'unconventional' methods, but after the preliminary session, in which she is brought to a thunderous climax – her first – she is more than willing to complete the course . . .

0 7515 1342 3

## DARES
**Roxanne Morgan**

It began over lunch. Three different women, best friends, decide to spice up their love-lives with a little extra-curricular sex. Shannon is first, accepting the dare of seducing a motorcycle despatch rider – while riding pillion through the streets of London.

The others follow, Nadia and Corey, hesitant at first but soon willing to risk all in the pursuit of new experiences and the heady thrill of trying to out-do each other's increasingly outrageous dares . . .

0 7515 1341 5

## SHOPPING AROUND
**Mariah Greene**

For Karen Taylor, special promotions manager in an upmarket Chelsea department store, choice of product is a luxury she enjoys just as much as her customers.

Richard – virile and vain; Alan – mature and cabinet-minister-sexy; and Maxwell, the androgynous boy supermodel who's fronting her latest campaign. Sooner or later, Karen's going to have to decide between these and others. But when you're shopping around, sampling the goods is half the fun . . .

0 7515 1459 4

# DARK SECRET
## Marina Anderson

Harriet Radcliffe was bored with her life. At twenty-three, her steady job and safe engagement suddenly seemed very dull. If she was to inject a little excitement into her life, she realised, now was the time to do it.

But the excitement that lay in store was beyond even her wildest ambitions. Answering a job advertisement to assist a world-famous actress, Harriet finds herself plunged into an intense, enclosed world of sexual obsession – playing an unwitting part in a very private drama, but discovering in the process more about her own desires than she had ever dreamed possible . . .

0 7515 1490 X

| [ ] | Back in Charge | Mariah Greene | £4.99 |
| [ ] | The Discipline of Pearls | Susan Swann | £4.99 |
| [ ] | Hotel Aphrodisia | Dorothy Starr | £4.99 |
| [ ] | Arousing Anna | Nina Sheridan | £4.99 |
| [ ] | Playing the Game | Selina Seymour | £4.99 |
| [ ] | The Women's Club | Vanessa Davies | £4.99 |
| [ ] | A Slave to His Kiss | Anastasia Dubois | £4.99 |
| [ ] | Saturnalia | Zara Devereux | £4.99 |
| [ ] | Shopping Around | Mariah Greene | £4.99 |
| [ ] | Dares | Roxanne Morgan | £4.99 |
| [ ] | Dark Secret | Marina Anderson | £4.99 |

X Libris offers an eXciting range of quality titles which can be ordered from the following address:

Little, Brown and Company (UK),
P.O. Box 11,
Falmouth,
Cornwall TR10 9EN

Alternatively you may fax your order to the above address.
FAX No. 01326 376423.

Payments can be made as follows: cheque, postal order (payable to Little, Brown and Company) or by credit cards, Visa/Access. Do not send cash or currency. UK customers and B.F.P.O. please allow £1.00 for postage and packing for the first book, plus 50p for the second book, plus 30p for each additional book up to a maximum charge of £3.00 (7 books plus).

Overseas customers including Ireland please allow £2.00 for the first book plus £1.00 for the second book, plus 50p for each additional book.

NAME (Block Letters) _____

_____

ADDRESS _____

_____

_____

☐  I enclose my remittance for _____

☐  I wish to pay by Access/Visa card

Number _____ Card Expiry Date _____